THE MASKED MARKSMAN:
CURTAIN CALL FOR THE CORPSE

AND OTHER STORIES

CURTAIN CALL FOR THE CORPSE

AND OTHER STORIES

By Emile C. Tepperman

POPULAR PUBLICATIONS • 2026

PUBLISHING HISTORY

"Curtain Call for the Corpse" originally appeared in the May, 1939 (Vol. 17, No. 4) issue of *The Spider* magazine. "A Cue for the Corpse" originally appeared in the August, 1939 (Vol. 18, No. 3) issue of *The Spider* magazine. "Headliner From Hell" originally appeared in the October, 1939 (Vol. 19, No. 1) issue of *The Spider* magazine. "Death's Booking Agent" originally appeared in the June, 1940 (Vol. 21, No. 1) issue of *The Spider* magazine. "Bank-Night for Corpses" originally appeared in the July, 1940 (Vol. 21, No. 2) issue of *The Spider* magazine. "Murder's One-Man Show" originally appeared in the August, 1940 (Vol. 21, No. 3) issue of *The Spider* magazine.

Visit POPULARPUBLICATIONS.com for more books like this.

"The Masked Marksman" logo courtesy of Chris Kalb.

CURTAIN CALL FOR THE CORPSE

FROM WHERE he sat, Ed Race could command a view of the entrance to the restaurant, as well as of the street beyond the ornate plate-glass windows. Lambini's was crowded tonight.

Most of the people who had spent the winter in Florida were back in town, and patronizing the theaters, enthusiastically. After the show, the place to go was Lambini's. Everybody who was anybody drifted in there off Times Square at some time during the course of the night. In addition, a goodly portion of the guests of the two-thousand-room Pemberton Hotel, of which Lambini's Rotisserie occupied the entire ground floor, took their meals here.

Ed ordered clam chowder and frog's legs, and turned his attention to the patrons of the restaurant. Any one of them might be the person who had sent him the telegram he now had in his pocket. It had been delivered to him at the Clyde Theater a half hour ago, just after his act was over. A property man had given it to him as he came off the stage, and it read:

> LAMBINI'S AT MIDNIGHT. A TABLE NEAR THE SIDE-STREET EXIT. SIT FACING THE BROADWAY ENTRANCE. BRING ALONG THE ARTILLERY.
>
> A FRIEND OF BINGO.

THE MASKED MARKSMAN

Simultaneously, the two guns spoke!

The evening newspaper which Ed had just bought before coming into the restaurant carried big black headlines about Bingo. But the newspapers and the police knew him by another name—Barry Payne.

"Barry Payne Escapes From State Prison!" screamed the headline, and underneath it:

EX-VAUDEVILLE ACROBAT ESCAPES BY SWINGING THIRTY FEET OVER JAIL WALL ON ROPE SUSPENDED FROM PRISON ROOF! HAD SERVED SIX YEARS OF FIFTEEN YEAR SENTENCE FOR WOUNDING ACE CADOGAN, GAMBLER.

There were two columns, and several pictures. Ed Race's picture was among them. He had been Barry Payne's best friend. They had toured vaudeville circuits throughout the country for years, each in a separate act, but frequently appearing on the same bill. Barry Payne had been billed as "THE FLYING YANK." He took tremendous risks on the swinging trapeze, never working with a net. It was that agility of his, Ed reflected, which had enabled him to escape from prison tonight.

Ed Race, himself, was billed as "The Masked Marksman—the Man Who Can Make Guns Talk." A great friendship had sprung up between Ed and Barry. "Bingo" was the nickname Ed had for him. It was a personal nickname between them, so Ed Race knew that the person who had sent the telegram was really a friend of Barry Payne's. The "artillery" of course, referred to the heavy .45 caliber, hair-trigger revolvers which were part of the six weapons used in the Masked Marksman's number. Ed had two of those guns in his shoulder holsters now.

He looked at his wristwatch. It was ten minutes before midnight.

THE MASKED MARKSMAN

A MAN came into the restaurant and stood at the door for a long minute, letting his keen, hawk-like eyes travel from table to table until he spotted Ed Race. Ed frowned. Of all the men he knew, this one was the last he wanted to encounter tonight. Inspector MacSpain, dour and grim, boss of the Broadway squad, was a hard man to fool.

MacSpain smiled tightly and threaded his way among the tables. Without asking permission, he seated himself in the vacant chair facing Ed.

"I was looking for you," he said. "I tried Dempsey's, and Gitlow's, and then I looked in here."

"What's on your mind, Mac?" Ed asked.

MacSpain studied him with piercing, shrewd eyes. "You know what's on my mind, Ed. Barry Payne is a friend of yours. He escaped from state prison today. The chances are ninety-nine out of a hundred that he'll be heading back toward New York. He'll need money and help."

Ed Race was poker-faced. "So what?" he asked.

"So this," MacSpain said grimly. "It's almost a sure bet that Barry Payne will try to get in touch with you somehow. What are you going to do—help him, or turn him in?"

Ed Race's eyes met those of the older man. "What would *you* do in my place, Mac?"

MacSpain lowered his eyes first. He sighed. "I was afraid of that, Ed." He stood up. "We've been friends a long time, and I know how you feel about Barry Payne. But I'm a police officer. So you can't blame me if I put a tail on you. I'm going to have you shadowed twenty-four hours a day—until Payne is caught.

Any move you make to help him—I'll know it. And I'll have to place you in custody."

Ed Race gave him a twisted smile. "So it's to be war, Mac?"

The inspector nodded. "For your sake, I hope Payne doesn't try to communicate with you. It'll only lay you open to a charge of harboring a fugitive from justice."

MacSpain stalked out of the restaurant. Ed watched his broad, unyielding back, and saw him talk to two men, out in the street. Ed knew both of them—Tyler and Hemming, two of the keenest plainclothesmen attached to the Broadway squad. MacSpain spoke only a few words to the two detectives, and then left them. Tyler remained on Broadway, in front of the restaurant, and Hemming came inside, selected a table not far from Ed's. He gave Ed a thin, unfriendly smile, and proceeded to order a cup of coffee in a loud rasping voice.

Ed's clam chowder arrived. He looked at it sourly. He stole a glance at his watch. Midnight. The appointment here had become a trap for Barry Payne.

Without appetite he began to eat the chowder. It was excellent, savory. But he didn't enjoy it. Lambini's made a specialty of clam chowder. They served it in a deep bowl containing almost a pint of the thick, luscious soup. It was fifty cents a bowl, and well worth it.

But Ed hardly knew what he was eating. If only he could guess who this friend of Bingo's was, he might warn him. For it was certain that MacSpain's men would shadow anyone who contacted Ed tonight.

Ordinarily, the police were inclined to work with Ed Race.

The salary which he received for his gun-juggling act, under the name of the Masked Marksman, was sufficient to provide him with everything he needed in life—except excitement. His high-strung nature required something more than the adulation and applause he found in the theater. So he had adopted a hobby—that of criminology. He held licenses to operate as a private detective in a dozen states, and he was always ready to place his services at the disposal of acquaintances in trouble. In the case of Barry Payne he had far more than an academic interest. For Barry was more than an acquaintance.

SUDDENLY, ED'S eyes narrowed. A woman he knew had just entered the restaurant. Nina Cadogan—the wife of Ace Cadogan. She was slender and lithe, with a thin, perfectly-contoured face that might have graced the costliest cameo of the Renaissance. What was she doing here, tonight of all nights—the wife of the man whom Barry Payne had shot six years ago?

Nina Cadogan looked around the crowded restaurant much as Inspector MacSpain had done a few minutes past—with this difference, that she had rather the look of a frightened doe than of a hunter of men such as MacSpain was. She found Ed Race with her glance. There was a sudden tensing of her features, and she started to make her way directly toward him.

In a flash Ed Race realized the situation. *Nina Cadogan was the friend of Bingo!*

He glanced sideways at Hemming. The dapper Broadway detective was eyeing Nina Cadogan with a queer mixture of suspicion and puzzlement.

She reached Ed's table and slipped into the seat opposite him.

She was even more beautiful at close range than at a distance. Ed remembered when she had been a musical comedy star. He had known her pretty well, in those days, and so had Barry Payne. Barry had taken her out a lot. Then one day she married Ace Cadogan, the gambler—Ace Cadogan, who controlled the gambling racket in New York with an iron hand, and who had enough money even in those days to give her anything she might want.

Two years after she married Cadogan, Barry Payne had walked into a police station one night and nonchalantly informed the desk sergeant that he had just shot Ace Cadogan. Nobody had connected Nina with the possible motive at that time. Barry's story was that he got into an argument with Cadogan about a gambling debt, and shot him. Cadogan, when he came out of the hospital, told the same story. Barry's confession was enough. He got fifteen years.

Ed faced her across the table, and his eyes narrowed speculatively. He wondered now if there hadn't been some other motive behind that shooting....

Nina Cadogan put a slim hand across the table.

"Ed!" she breathed. "I sent you that telegram. You—you'll help Barry, won't you?"

"Careful, Nina," he started to say. "We're being watched—"

And then he broke off, because he felt her pressing something into his hand.

"Take it!" she said urgently. "It's the key to Room Sixteen-sixteen in the hotel upstairs. Barry is there. He won't open for anyone. Just use the key."

Ed palmed it. It was a small key, with a pressed-metal tag attached to it, probably bearing the room number. He just felt it, but didn't dare open his hand to look at it, under Hemming's eyes.

"What happened?" he asked Nina Cadogan. "Why did Barry do such a desperate thing? He would have been eligible to parole in three years more."

There was haunting terror in her eyes. "He wouldn't wait. He—he wants to kill Ace—my husband. God help me, I arranged his escape. But I didn't know that was the reason he wanted to get out. I—I thought he'd take passage on a freighter that I arranged for him, and go to South America. But—but he came to New York instead. He swears he'll kill Ace and then give himself up again."

Ed looked at her keenly. "Why? Why does he want to kill Ace Cadogan? And why did *you* arrange his escape?"

"Because I love him!" she said simply. Then she leaned forward, a bright flush coloring her cameo-white skin. "Go upstairs and see him, Ed. For God's sake, make him give up that mad idea of killing Ace. Make him take the boat—leave the country."

Ed laughed bitterly. "There isn't much chance. MacSpain's men are shadowing me. And from now on they'll be shadowing you—"

He froze into silence at a warning glance from her. He turned and saw that Hemming had risen from his table and was coming toward them very purposefully.

Nina Cadogan spoke swiftly, rushing her words. "I'll lead him away, Ed—take him off your trail. Then you can go see Barry. Good-by. Good luck!"

She pushed back her chair, got up, and turned and ran toward the Broadway door. Her intention was apparent. She hoped, by acting so, to make Hemming take after her. But she didn't know about Tyler. And Hemming didn't rise to the bait. He stopped alongside Ed, and grinned.

"Nice going, Race. Tyler will get the Cadogan dame. And it looks like I'm in luck. She handed you something over the table. Can't fool old Eagle Eye. Maybe it's a message from Barry Payne, eh? Maybe it's the address of his hideout." He thrust out a hand, palm up. "Give!"

OUT OF the corner of his eye, Ed saw that Nina Cadogan had stopped near the door. She was not looking back, but was facing two men who had just come in. One of them was Inspector MacSpain. The other was Ace Cadogan—Nina's husband.

Just behind Cadogan was another man—a big hulk of a fellow, with a gorilla-like face, flat nose, and big ears that were battered around into little cauliflower ridges. That was Joey Gluck, one-time ham prize-fighter, who, after being barred from the ring, had gotten the job of bodyguard to Ace Cadogan. Joey Gluck had very few whole bones in his hands, so his fists weren't much good. But he could use a gun very well, and rumor had it that he had performed several executions ordered by Cadogan.

Ace Cadogan had grabbed Nina by the arm, and was leading her back to the table. MacSpain came along, smirking. Joey Gluck brought up the rear. Dozens of patrons craned their necks to see what was happening, but when Joey scowled at them they hastily looked away.

The small group reached Ed's table. Cadogan spoke first. He was tall and thin, and his eyes were closely spaced, narrow and black. His mouth was a thin scar in a pale, emotionless face. His long hard fingers were pressing painfully into Nina's arm. She was biting her lip to repress an expression of pain.

"Let's see what's been going on here," Cadogan said tauntingly. "I didn't know you were making a play for my wife."

Hemming didn't let him go on. He blurted, "Inspector! Mrs. Cadogan came in and talked to Race. She gave him something. I think it's a message from Payne. Maybe the location of his hideout. There—" he pointed—"Race just put it in his pocket!"

Cadogan's thin lips twisted into a mocking smile. "Well, what do you know about that!" he said to Nina. "So you've been in touch with Payne all these years! And helping him escape from jail, too. Well, well."

MacSpain pushed Cadogan out of the way and faced Ed Race.

"I'm going to search you, Ed. I want that thing that Mrs. Cadogan gave you."

Ed shook his head. "You know you can't search me, Mac. You know you've got to arrest a man before you can search him."

"Then I'll arrest you. I can charge you with suspicion of harboring a fugitive." His voice was almost pleading. "Don't make me arrest you, Ed."

Suddenly Ed nodded. "All right, Mac. I'll let you search me."

For the first time since returning into the restaurant, Nina Cadogan spoke.

"No, no!" she cried. "You can't—"

She became silent at a glance from Ed. Her eyes were agonized, seeking some reassurance from him that MacSpain would not find the hotel key on him.

MacSpain stepped quickly to Ed's side and thrust a hand into the pocket that Hemming had indicated. He brought out a package of cigarettes and a book of matches—nothing else. He opened the matchbook, and tore apart the cigarette package. He found nothing.

He turned a heavy glance on Hemming now.... "Are you sure he put it in that pocket?"

Hemming shrugged. "Maybe he just put his hand in his pocket to fool me. Maybe he ditched that thing." He got down on his knees, and searched the floor all around the table. Then he moved all the plates on the table, and lifted up the table cloth.

"It's not here, Inspector. He must have it on him some place. His hands move so fast, he might have put it in one of his other pockets."

MacSpain nodded. "We'll go in the men's room, Ed."

Together, they made their way toward the rear. Nina Cadogan watched them, full of anxiety and fear—Ace Cadogan, sneeringly; Detective Hemming, puzzledly; Joey Gluck, gloweringly.

At last the door of the washroom closed behind Ed Race and Inspector MacSpain. The group waited in silence. Tyler came in from outside and joined them. All eyes in the restaurant were focused on them.

Hemming turned and said to Nina Cadogan, "You *did* give him something, didn't you?"

She pressed her lips tightly together, lowered her eyes.

Ace Cadogan, still gripping her arm, laughed bitingly. "You wouldn't want Nina to incriminate herself, would you, Hemming?" He turned to her, and his close-set black eyes burned hatefully. "But you'll tell me all about it when we get back to the club, won't you, Nina, darling?"

She shuddered, but did not reply.

After what seemed an eternity of time, the door of the men's room at the rear opened, and MacSpain came out first, followed by Ed Race.

Nina Cadogan grew tense. She watched the two men hungrily, as if trying to read from their faces whether the key had been found on Ed.

The two men came up to the table, and MacSpain grimaced at Hemming. "You must have been mistaken. I searched him down to the skin. He hasn't a thing on him."

Nina Cadogan expelled a great sigh of relief, while her eyes reflected puzzled wonder.

Ace Cadogan shrugged. "In that case, I guess you won't want Nina any more. If you should, you'll find her with me at the club."

He started to lead her away. She held back. "I—I think—"

"Never mind what you think!" Cadogan snarled at her. "You're coming with me!"

When they left, MacSpain said, "I'm sure she did give you something, Race. She's tied up with Barry Payne in some way.

She tipped you off where he's hiding out. And I'm sorry for her. When that fiend of a husband of hers gets to working on her...." He shrugged. "It's no skin off *my* teeth. Maybe he'll make her tell where Payne is holing up. As for you, Ed, I'm keeping you shadowed every minute. Don't forget it."

He nodded to Tyler and Hemming, and went out after Cadogan and Nina.

Ed smiled engagingly at Hemming. "Too bad, old man—"

He made an awkward motion with his hand, and struck the bowl of clam chowder, which was still on the table. It went hurtling off to the floor, and Ed uttered an exclamation of dismay, stepped backward and tripped over the chair. He fell to the floor, almost in the mess of clam chowder.

Swiftly his hand felt around on the floor until he touched the hotel key, which he had dropped into the bowl when MacSpain had offered to search him. He palmed the key and scrambled to his feet, looking ruefully down at his coat and trousers, which were spattered with soup.

"I guess I better go inside and clean up," he muttered, and made for the men's room. Hemming hesitated a moment, then followed him, while Tyler remained at the table.

Ed entered the men's room, with Hemming close behind him.

"I'm sticking to you, pal!" Hemming said. "There's a back door out of this men's room, into the hotel lobby. I'm not letting you cop a sneak on me."

Ed said, "Thanks for the information, Hemming. I had some such idea myself." And he brought up his right fist in a short crackling arc to the point of Hemming's chin.

The detective's head snapped back, a little grunt escaped him, and he gently folded up. Ed caught him, eased him down to the floor, and hurried out the back door, into the lobby of the Pemberton Hotel.

HE TOOK the elevator up to the sixteenth floor. He inserted the key in the door of 1616, and pushed inside. The room was dark, the shades down. He could see nothing. He closed the door behind him, and groped for a light switch. Suddenly a flashlight from somewhere in the center of the room beamed into brilliance, spotting him.

A voice said, "Stand still!" and then, almost at once, "Ed! Good God, I thought you wouldn't come!"

Ed grinned into the flashlight, and flicked on the light switch.

Barry Payne was sitting on the bed. He put away the gun and flashlight and sprang across the room, took Ed's hands in both of his.

Barry Payne was slim and wiry. He was handsome, with dark curly hair, and a straight, patrician nose. But his cheeks were pale, sunken from his long years of confinement. He was nervous and tense, too.

Ed put a hand on his shoulder. "Bingo! Why did you do it? You could have got paroled in three years, and come back and lived like a man—instead of being hunted like this."

Barry Payne slumped on the bed. "I've come back to kill Cadogan," he muttered.

Ed Race stared down at him, frowning. "Do you hate him so much, Bingo? You tried to kill him once, six years ago. Why not let it rest?"

Payne raised stricken eyes to his friend. "No, Ed. I—I didn't try to kill him six years ago. I—didn't—shoot—Cadogan!"

Ed's eyes narrowed. Slowly he sat down on the bed next to Payne.

"Say that again, Barry."

"It's the truth, Ed."

"But you walked into the station house and confessed," Ed insisted. "You took the blame for it. My God, Barry, why have you kept silent for six years? If you had told me that in the first place, I'd have gone out and found the guilty party—"

Payne smiled at him twistedly. "That's just what I didn't want you to do, Ed. That's why I kept silent—even with you. I—I know who the guilty party is!"

"Nina Cadogan!" Ed breathed.

Barry Payne nodded.

"That evening—" his voice was charged with emotion brought to him by remembrance of that night six years ago—"I went to see Nina at their home. I loved Nina. She was going to ask Ace Cadogan for a divorce. We were going to tell him frankly that we loved each other. I found the door open, and I heard Joey Gluck's voice inside, talking over the telephone. He was saying, 'For Gawd's sake, doc, hurry over. The boss has been shot!'

"I pushed the door open a little, and saw Cadogan on the floor, unconscious. I didn't go in. I went away. Downstairs, I saw Nina. She was walking up and down in front of the building, and she looked nervous. I didn't let her see me. I went out the back way. I knew what had happened. She had started to tell Ace Cadogan about me, not waiting for me to get there. And he must have taunted her, perhaps struck her. Then she must have shot him. And she was waiting down there to tell me about it."

Barry Payne buried his head in his hands. "God, Ed, you don't know what it means to think of the woman you love going to jail. She wouldn't have got any mercy, especially when the jury learned that she loved another man. And Cadogan would have seen to it that the jury learned everything."

Ed Race nodded, somberly. "I can understand that, Bingo. Cadogan is a sadist. He enjoys making her suffer. I saw that in the restaurant tonight."

Barry's fists clenched. "He still does that. I know it. She as much as told me so, the last time she visited me in jail. That's why I made her help me escape. The last thing I do in this life will be to free her from Ace Cadogan! I'll do that now!"

Ed put a hand on his shoulder. "Take it easy, Bingo. What did you do after you saw her walking up and down in front of the building?"

"I couldn't let her take the rap for it," the other said. "So I headed her off. I went to the station house and gave myself up, and said that it was I who had shot Cadogan. I hoped Cadogan would let it ride like that. I hoped he'd be satisfied with seeing me punished. And he did. When he came out of the hospital, he told the same story I had told. You know the rest."

Ed was silent for a long time. Then he asked in a strange voice, "And Nina—she let you make the sacrifice? She didn't object?"

"She never spoke about it. It must have been a devilish shock to her. You know how some people are—they can't bring themselves to speak about certain things that have shocked their nervous systems."

Suddenly, Barry Payne jerked to his feet. "That's all there is to it, Ed. Now I'm going." He hefted the gun in his hand. "There are seven slugs in this automatic. I'll put six of them into Ace Cadogan's body—make sure I kill him this time. And the seventh is for me. I had to see you before I went through with it, though. I couldn't kick the bucket having you think the wrong thing about me. Now you know. Take care of Nina. She'll be a widow—and probably broke, because Cadogan's gambling racket will topple when he passes. You'll look after her, Ed?"

Ed Race got to his feet. "Yes, Bingo. I'll look after her. And after you, too, you damned Quixotic fool!"

Payne stared at him. "What do you mean?"

"This!" said Ed.

For the second time that evening he hit a man. He gave Barry Payne everything he had, right on the button.

His blow practically lifted Payne off his feet and deposited him sprawling unconscious, on the bed.

Ed caressed his knuckles and looked down affectionately upon his inert friend.

"Sorry I had to do that to you, Bingo," he murmured. "But you need a guardian. I guess I'm it!"

HE TOOK one of the pillow-cases off the bed, and tore it into strips. He started to tie Barry Payne's hands, when the 'phone at the bedside rang with an alarming jangle. He looked at it for a moment, frowning. Then he shrugged, picked it up.

"Ed!" the voice was that of Nina Cadogan, charged with terror. "You have to get him out of there;—quick!"

"Wait a minute, Nina," Ed said. "I want to ask you something first—"

"But there's not time, Ed—"

"This is important," Ed insisted. "Barry is at the end of his rope. He was crazy to come to New York. Now there isn't a chance in a thousand of his getting out. They'll surely catch him, sooner or later. And he'll have years added to his sentence for the jail break. There's only one way to save him—that's to prove him innocent."

"I—I don't understand," she quavered.

"If the person who really shot your husband were to come forward and admit it, it would mean that Barry was innocent in the first place, and he'd rate a full pardon. The jail break wouldn't be held against him."

"But—but Ed! Barry *did* shoot Ace—"

"How do you know?" he demanded.

"He admitted it."

"Didn't *you* shoot Ace?" he asked.

"I?" There was a moment of tense silence. Then, "Ed! Is Barry there? Does he say he didn't do it?"

"Barry is here. He tells me he took the blame because he thought *you* had done it. He saw you outside the building that night—"

"Oh, God!" the words coming over the wire seemed to be torn from her throat. "And I thought Barry had done it! Ed, I swear to you, I didn't shoot Ace. I had just come home, and I heard a pistol shot. Then I heard Ace cry out. I—I thought Barry shot him. So I ran out. I watched in the street, waiting for Barry to come out, so I could warn him if the police were coming. But he never appeared. He must have left by the back way. The next thing I knew, he had surrendered."

Ed Race groaned. "You two little fools! Keeping silent all these years, and letting each other think in circles!"

"But, Ed—*who* did it?"

"I don't know. I'm going to find out—"

"There's no time!" Her voice rose shrilly as she thought of the reason why she had called. "You must get Barry out of there. Ace took me back here to the club and beat me. Then he went through my handbag, and found the duplicate key to that room. He—he guessed that Barry is there. He sent Joey Gluck to kill Barry!"

"To *kill* him?" Ed frowned. "Why? All he had to do was to notify MacSpain."

"I don't know what's in his mind. I—"

Above the sound of Nina's words in the receiver, Ed caught another sound. A key was being gently inserted in the lock. His eyes leaped to the doorknob, saw it turning slowly.

"Hang up, Nina!" he whispered into the 'phone. He clicked down the receiver, replaced the instrument and snatched up the strips with which he had been about to tie Barry Payne. Then he leaped across into the bathroom. He was only just in time. The door began to open slowly. The bathroom was dark, and Ed was in shadow. He saw Joey Gluck come into the room.

JOEY CAME in stealthily, a gun in a gloved hand. His gorilla-face was twisted into an expression of extreme slyness. When he saw Barry Payne on the bed, he exhaled a breath of satisfaction.

Ed tensed, thinking Gluck might shoot Barry at once. But instead, Joey tiptoed over to the bed and looked down at Barry, then bent over and listened to see if he was breathing.

Ed watched with narrowed eyes. Gluck picked up Barry Payne's limp right hand and placed it around the stock of the gun he had brought with him. He pushed Barry's forefinger over the trigger. Then he turned Barry's hand and the gun, so that the muzzle was close to Barry's right temple.

Then Ed Race came out of the bathroom. Two quick steps brought him behind the gunman. Joey Gluck must have sensed his presence. He whirled, leaving the gun in Barry's hand. His own hand streaked up to his shoulder holster. But Ed Race's big .45 was already boring into his side.

Gluck's mouth dropped open. He let his gun slide back in its holster, and slowly raised his hands.

Ed gave him a grin. He dipped in and took Joey's gun out of the holster.

"Turn around and lie down on your face on the floor," he ordered.

Joey Gluck looked into Ed's eyes.

He got to his knees, and then stretched out on his face on the rug. Ed straddled him and tied his wrists with the strips of pillow-case. Then he tied his ankles, and ran the strip to the bedpost, tying one end there. But he intentionally made it long enough, so Joey could get almost to the head of the bed.

"Funny," he said, taking the gun out of Barry Payne's limp hand. "You bringing a gun to plant on Barry and make it look like he killed himself. Wouldn't it have been easier to tip the cops to this room?"

Joey didn't answer.

"And how come you went ahead and used this gun, when Barry's own gun was lying here on the bed?"

He saw that Joey had turned his head and was looking up at him queerly. Ed could read the gunman's mind. Joey was wondering if Ed would forget to gag him. Ed said, "Well, so long, Joey. Be seeing you in about twenty minutes."

He backed out of the room, closing the door behind him. In the hall he almost bumped into Inspector MacSpain.

THE INSPECTOR laughed grimly. "Joey Gluck led me here without knowing it. That guy is too dumb to spot a good tail. I got the floor from the elevator operator, and what do I see when I get off, but you, backing out of a room!" Abruptly, MacSpain's tone grew ominous. "I'm sorry, Ed, but if Barry Payne is in that room, I'll have to arrest you."

Ed Race broke in, talking impetuously. "Give me a five minute break, Mac. Come on downstairs. I'll explain on the way. Inside of five minutes I hope to clear the whole thing up. Barry Payne never shot Cadogan, in the first place!"

They took the down elevator, and on the way Ed told him about Joey Gluck in the room. "I gave him just enough rope to reach the 'phone alongside the bed. He can knock it over and make a call. I hope to heaven he isn't too dumb to think of it!"

He rushed MacSpain across the lobby to the telephone switchboard, and got MacSpain to show his badge to the girl.

"Is there a call coming through from sixteen-sixteen?" he demanded.

She pointed to one of the lights on the board. "Just asked for a number," she told him. "Edgeware Four-one-four-one-four."

Ed's eyes flashed. "That's the Club Cadogan! Plug us in so we can listen!"

She took off her earphones. Ed and MacSpain put their heads together, each listening in on one of them. The connection had already been established, and they could hear the cold voice of Ace Cadogan.

"What's the trouble, Joey?" came the question.

"For Gawd's sake, boss, you better come up and get me, quick. That mug Race got the drop on me and he's got me tied up like a mummy. Only the sap forgot to gag me and I managed to knock over the 'phone—"

"What about Payne?" Cadogan asked. "Did he get away?"

"No. He's right here on the bed," Gluck said. "He's out cold. I started to work on him. I put the gun in his hand, and before I could give it to him, this guy Race jumped me—"

"Did Race get the gun?"

"Yeah," said Joey. "And the cops have the bullet that was taken outa you, six years ago. If they check it with this gun they'll see it's the same—"

"Shut up, you fool! You're on an open wire. I'll be right over!"

Inspector MacSpain put down the earphones and took a deep breath. "Boy! Then Payne didn't shoot him!" he said.

"I think," Ed said, "that there must have been an accident that night. Joey Gluck may have shot Cadogan by accident. Or Cadogan may have shot himself. Then, when Barry confessed, he practically framed himself for them."

"How is Cadogan going to get in that room now?" MacSpain asked.

Ed grinned. "I left the key in the door. I made it as easy for him as I could. The Club Cadogan is only around the corner. He ought to be here in a couple of minutes. I'm going upstairs. You stay down here and take the next elevator after him."

MacSpain nodded, and Ed left him. He hurried upstairs and went into 1616.

Joey Gluck had worked around on his back now, and the telephone was lying on the floor beside him. He had somehow managed to get the receiver back on the hook.

Barry Payne was beginning to stir on the bed, but he was not yet fully conscious.

Ed said, "I just came back to see how you're making out, pal." He pretended not to notice the telephone. "I have to go out again. I'll be back soon."

"Go on and scram!" Gluck spat out. "See if I care!"

Ed grinned. "Turn around on your face again—or I'll smack you!"

Gluck complied sullenly. Ed pulled a blanket out from under Barry Payne and threw it over the gunman's head.

"So long, Joey," he sang out. He went noisily to the door, opened it and scraped his feet, then slammed it shut again. But he remained inside, and swung into the bathroom.

As soon as the door closed, Joey Gluck shucked the blanket off him. He started to struggle with his bonds, swearing.

After three or four minutes of this, the corridor door opened. Gluck looked up eagerly. "Gawd, boss, I couldn't help it—"

ACE CADOGAN came into the room. Behind him was another man, smaller and thinner than Cadogan, with the pinched features of a cokey. Ed knew that other one. He was Sam Coney, a professional killer.

Coney kicked the door shut and leaned against it, with a gun in his hand. Ace Cadogan also had a small, gun-metal automatic. He looked down at Gluck.

"You're too damn dumb, Joey," he said softly. "That time when you shot me by accident, I let it go because it was a chance to frame Payne. But now you go and get yourself in a mess. Race saw you here and tied you up. He got that old gun of yours too, that you were going to plant on Payne. Where do you think he went?"

Joey Gluck was watching him with slowly widening eyes. "To—to the cops?"

"Exactly!" Cadogan smiled grimly. "This is the first time the cops will have anything on you. I've always planned things for you so you would be in the clear. Now they can take you downtown and sweat you. And you'll open up about a dozen other things, because you can't take sweating any more."

"Gawd, boss, I been loyal—"

Cadogan shrugged. "Loyal but dumb. Now you're dangerous to me. So Coney here is going to give it to you, and to Payne while he's still out. Then we'll untie you. It'll look like some sort of scrap between you two." He now smiled crookedly.

Coney had a silencer on his gun. He spat on the rug, grinned, and lifted the gun.

Joey Gluck suddenly screamed hoarsely, "Wait—"

And Ed Race appeared from the bathroom. He had no guns in his hands, which were swinging loosely at his sides.

"That would be murder," he said.

Ace Cadogan and Sam Coney spun around at the sound of his voice. Both their guns swung toward him viciously. Cadogan was at his right, Coney at his left. Their slugs would crisscross in his body.

Ed Race's hands moved with such blinding speed that they seemed not to move at all. But those two heavy forty-fives appeared by some uncanny magic.

He did that trick every day on the stage for the benefit of the audiences of the Follies. Each night he would come on the stage and send four china balls juggling high in the air. Then he would wait until they came down close to the floor. At the moment when the audience thought that they would surely fall to the ground, his two guns were out and roaring, and those four little balls would be smashed.

Now he did the same trick, with his life at stake. He did not uncross his hands over his chest. He fired the right-hand gun at Coney, the left hand one at Cadogan. Both men fell before they could pull the triggers of their own guns. It is doubtful if either knew what hit them. But they were both dead.

And on the heels of the shots a terrific pounding was set up on the door. Ed reached over and opened it, and MacSpain came barging into the room.

"You did a good job, Ed," he muttered.

Ed nodded. "I think you'll get all you want from Gluck. He ought to talk his head off. I just saved his life."

Barry Payne was stirring on the bed, with his eyes open. He was staring uncomprehendingly at the scene. He raised a hand and felt of his jaw, then looked accusingly at Ed.

"Why did you hit me?" he asked.

Ed grinned. "I wanted to be sure you wouldn't hog the credit for shooting Cadogan this time. As soon as the red tape is all cut, you can go and get Nina. And then you can spend the rest of your lives telling each other what saps you've both been for the last six years!"

A CUE FOR THE CORPSE

ED RACE heard the little *bang* while he was shaving, but he paid no attention to it. It might have been the backfire of any one of the ten thousand cars passing on Broadway, eight floors below; or it might have been a guest in one of the other rooms committing suicide—or getting murdered. Whatever it was, Ed didn't intend to investigate.

There was a midnight show at the Clyde Theater tonight, and his act was due at one-ten. It was eleven-thirty now, and he wanted to dress and eat before he went on. So he finished shaving, and then went into the bedroom and put on his shirt and tie and vest.

Over the vest he strapped the twin shoulder-holsters containing the two heavy .45 caliber hair-trigger revolvers which he used in his gun-juggling and marksmanship act. Then he put on his coat and hat and turned out the light. With the light out in the room, all the glittering incandescence of Broadway surged up through the window. Electric lights flickered and flashed from hundreds of huge signs. Two blocks down he could see the marquee of the Clyde Theater, where his own act was headlined:

THIS WEEK ONLY
THE MASKED MARKSMAN
THE MAN WHO CAN MAKE GUNS TALK!
IN PERSON!

Ed grinned at that. He was used to it now, though it had been a little thrilling for the first couple of years. It was ten years since he had first gone up in electric lights. And now he was the highest-paid performer on the Partages Circuit. He liked it. He liked to juggle those heavy guns, and bring down the house in thunderous applause when he shot out the flames of a dozen candles in succession, thirty feet across the stage. Every night it was a new thrill.

He pulled open the door and started to step out into the corridor. But he suddenly stopped with his hand on the knob, and said in surprise, "Well, for the love of Pete!"

There was a girl in the hall, and she was lugging a dead man by the feet!

SHE WAS hardly more than seventeen or eighteen, and her figure was slender and supple in a thin silk dress. She must have put it on in a hurry, because even in the dim light of the hallway it was easy to see that she wore nothing at all underneath it. And she had no shoes or stockings on, either.

He stared.

She was dragging the man by the feet. His shoulders bumped along the floor, and his arms did a crazy slithering act on the wine-colored rug. He was on his back, and there was a large black hole in his left temple. The blood was dried around the wound. His eyes were open and glazed, and his jaw hung slack. There was no doubt that he was dead.

The girl apparently had dragged him out of Room 814 across the hall, because the door of that room was ajar. When she heard Ed Race, she dropped the man's feet as if they were scorch-

The big .45s roared!

ing hot. Her eyes became wide and round. Her lower lip was trembling, and her small breasts were rising and falling with trip-hammer speed.

She stared at Ed Race without speaking.

Ed said gravely, "Why, you're only a kid. How come you're lugging a corpse? Don't you know you mustn't touch dead men till the police come?"

"I want to get rid of the body," she told him matter-of-factly.

"I guessed as much," he said dryly. "Who killed him?"

"I killed him."

Ed raised his eyebrows. "With what?"

"With a gun."

"Why?" he asked.

"Because he was no good. He's a gunman—Lefty Mott. I'm—I was his gun moll. We had a fight, and I shot him."

Ed looked at her thoughtfully. "A gun moll, eh? Aren't you a little young to be a gun moll?"

"I'm twenty-five!" she lied defiantly.

Ed grinned. "Twenty-five, eh? A pretty ripe old age at that. Do you mind telling me what you were going to do with Mr. Lefty Mott?"

"I was going to put him in the incinerator," she said.

"There isn't any incinerator here. This isn't a housekeeping hotel."

Her eyes widened. "But—but I thought every New York building had an incinerator."

"You haven't been in New York long, have you?" Ed asked.

"I have so! And I'm a moll, too. I'll prove it. Want me to prove it?"

"How?"

"Like this," she said.

She knelt swiftly beside the dead man, and thrust a hand inside his coat. She brought it out holding a huge automatic which she had taken from under the corpse's left armpit. It was so heavy she had to hold it in both hands as she pointed it at Ed.

"You do as I say," she blurted, "or I'll p-plug you like I plugged him. Get hold of his feet and pull him into your room!"

Just then they heard the clanging of the elevator doors around the bend in the corridor—and then voices, approaching. Two men were talking. One was whining, the other gruff and unyielding.

"I tell you, Inspector," Whiny was saying, "Inness plugged Lefty Mott right in his room. I seen him do it from my window across the street. He shot him in the head! And Lefty didn't even have a gun!"

The other voice was lower, but clear and authoritative. "All right, Gimp. We'll see for ourselves. There's an alarm out for Inness already. You better be giving me a straight steer, or it'll be just too bad for you!"

"Don't worry, Inspector. I know better than to try anything on you."

There was only a grunt from the Inspector.

Ed Race didn't recognize the whiny voice, but he certainly did know that other, authoritative voice. That would be Inspector Hansen, Chief of New York City Detectives. Hansen was a hard man, brilliant and unemotional. He and Ed Race had never been able to get along together.

Ed looked at the girl and saw that she was trembling. Her two hands were shaking so that the muzzle of the heavy automatic was wavering in a wide arc. If she fired it, she would be sure to hit anything but Ed. Also, Ed noticed with a grin that she didn't even know enough to snap off the safety catch. But she was holding to her bluff. Her voice assumed a villainous whisper.

"Hurry up and drag this corpse in there, or I'll—shoot!"

Ed said, "Well, well. I guess you've got me cold, sister." He whispered it so that the two men coming down the hall wouldn't hear. And then he took two steps forward, bent down and seized the defunct Mr. Lefty Mott by the feet, dragged mightily, and pulled him into the room.

THE GIRL uttered a deep sigh of relief and ran in after him. Ed swung the door shut just as Inspector Hansen and his stool-pigeon came around the bend of the corridor. He left the door open just a crack, so as to get a glimpse of them. Behind him he could hear the girl's quick, labored breathing.

Hansen and Gimp passed right by his room and went directly to the open door of 814.

Ed watched, saw Hansen look in, then turn and scowl at Gimp, without saying a word. Gimp looked, in his turn, and exclaimed, "My Gawd, Inspector, I swear I seen Lefty Mott get shot in there. Someone must have taken him out!"

Hansen said, "Yeah. I suppose they took him out through the whole hotel, and then down in the street, and just loaded him in a car, while all of Broadway watched!"

Gimp shrugged helplessly. "Maybe they dragged him in some other room on the floor—"

Hansen snapped his fingers. "You may be right at that! I'll call downtown and get some men. Then we'll search every room."

Very slowly and very carefully, Ed closed his door and locked it. He turned and faced the girl. She had heard what Hansen had said. She was staring at Ed, wide-eyed. She still held on to the automatic with both hands.

Ed smiled at her. "Well? You've got me in a nice jam now. When Hansen searches the floor he'll find this body here. And then he'll arrest me for murder."

There were tears in the girl's eyes. "I—I didn't want to do that to you. I—I only wanted to get rid of the body."

Ed put out his hand and took the automatic from her. She didn't resist. He turned it around and showed her the safety-catch.

"For a gun moll, you certainly are ignorant of firearms," he said. "In the future remember, if it's an automatic, it won't shoot unless you snap this little doo-dad."

He led her to a chair and sat her in it. "All right. Now suppose you tell me all about it. In the first place, I know you're not a gun moll. In the second place, I know you didn't kill Lefty Mott. In the third place, I know you're in a lot of trouble. Maybe I can help you out."

She sagged back helplessly in the chair and looked up at him with a pair of hopeless eyes. "Nobody can help me. You heard what they said in the hall. That man, Gimp, lied. He told the Inspector that my brother—that's Jack Inness—killed Lefty Mott. Well, Jack didn't kill him. I found Lefty dead in Jack's room, and I knew someone was trying to frame my brother, so I decided to drag the body out of there. I—"

She was interrupted by a heavy knock at the door. "Police Department!" a voice rasped. "Open up in there!"

Ed whispered to the girl, "That'll be Inspector Hansen. If he finds you here, your brother will be connected with the murder. All your trouble will be wasted. And if he finds me in here he'll surely take me downtown for questioning, and I won't be able to appear for my number at the Clyde Theater tonight."

Her eyes opened wide. "You—you're an actor?"

He nodded.

Hansen's knock was repeated, this time more loudly. "Open up, I say! I know there's someone in there. I know you've got a dead body in there. There's blood on the door-sill here!"

The girl was on her feet in a panic. "What—what'll we do?"

Ed leaped across to the closet, pulled one of his topcoats off a hanger, and threw it over her shoulders. "Put that on. You can't go out in the street in that thin dress."

He seized her arm, dragged her to the window. Hansen kept on knocking at the door. Now he was using the butt of his revolver. "Better open up. It'll go hard with you, whoever—"

The rest of his voice was lost because Ed had the window up and had already pushed the girl out onto the terrace, and in seconds he was out after her. He closed the window from the outside, leaving Lefty Mott in there all alone, in the majestic splendor of death.

The girl shrugged into the sleeves of the topcoat, and Ed led her all the way down to the end of the terrace. The next-to-the-last window along the terrace opened onto the corridor near the freight elevator shaft. Ed slid the window up, crawled in, the girl following. They were around the bend of the corridor now, and they could hear Hansen still hammering at the door.

Ed grinned and said, "I hope my friend the Inspector doesn't get high blood pressure over there!" He led her past the freight elevator doors to the fire-door. He pushed it open, and they both ran down the stairs to the seventh floor. On the seventh, Ed slowed up to a walk. He looked at the girl. "That's a man's topcoat you're wearing, but I guess it'll pass. Come on."

HE WENT to the passenger elevator shaft, and rang the down button. In a moment a cage arrived, and the door opened. Ed and the girl stepped in, and the elevator descended. The elevator operator said, "Hello, Mr. Race. What you doing on the seventh? I thought you was on the eighth."

"I had to pick up Miss Smith here," Ed told him.

"You missed some excitement," the operator said. "Seems like there's been a killing up on your floor. There's a police inspector up there, and he's going through all the rooms."

"Is that so?" Ed said. "I wonder who killed whom." He took a ten-dollar bill out of his pocket, folded it into a small wad and gave it to the operator. "Look, Sammy, do you think this would improve or spoil your memory?"

Sammy peeked at the denomination of the bill, and grinned. "It would make me suffer from amnesia, Mr. Race!"

"Okay. Just forget you saw me and Miss Smith. Oke?"

Sammy winked. "Oke." Suddenly he became doubtful. "But if it's murder—they can give you the chair for being accessory after the fact—"

"Don't worry, Sammy. I didn't do murder. Neither did Miss Smith."

"Well, Mr. Race, if you was to make it twenty—"

Ed sighed and took out another ten-dollar bill. "All right, Jesse James."

They were on the ground floor now, and Sammy grinned,

pocketed the extra ten, and opened the sliding door. Ed stepped out, holding the girl by the arm. He started to cross the lobby and then stopped, making a little grimace of disgust.

Three men had just come in, and were hurrying toward the elevators. "Those are Inspector Hansen's men," he told the girl. "Sergeant Bickert and two detectives. They'll tell Hansen they saw me coming out. And he'll learn that it's my room the body is in—"

The three men stopped directly in front of Ed and the girl.

Sergeant Bickert's eyes flicked swiftly over her, then swung to Ed. "Why hello, Mr. Masked Marksman. Fancy seeing you here—at a time when there's been a killing, too. Don't it beat everything how you're always around when there's a murder!"

Ed looked very innocent. "Murder, Bickert? Has someone been murdered in this hotel?"

Bickert was looking at him suspiciously. "Yeah. On the eighth floor. Might I ask, Mr. Race, what floor is *your* room on?"

Ed gave him a grin. "You might ask, Sergeant, but why should I reply? I have no intention of inviting you up for a drink. And now"—he took the girl's arm and started to push past the three detectives—"if you'll excuse me, Miss Smith and I have a little business to attend to."

Bickert put out an arm to bar his way. "Just a moment, Mr. Masked Marksman. This Miss Smith here—what is she, some kind of a back-to-nature girl?"

Ed scowled. "What do you mean?"

Bickert snickered. "I've heard of people walking barefoot in the country. But"—he shook his head sympathetically—"she's gonna find it tough walking on the pavement without shoes or stockings!"

For the first time Ed remembered that the girl was barefoot.

"Miss Smith is a toe dancer," he said stiffly. "She's joining my act tonight. She dances with two candles in her hair, and I shoot the candles. She always walks barefoot, to perfect her toe dancing."

"Well, well," said Bickert. "A toe dancer, huh? This whole business looks very interesting. Suppose we all go up to the eighth floor and talk to Inspector Hansen. I'm sure he'll be glad to see you."

The sergeant put out a big ham-like hand and took the girl's arm. "Come on, Miss Toe Dancer. We're going up. And you, too, Race!" He motioned to the two detectives, and they filed into Sammy's elevator.

Bickert jerked his head at Ed. "You next, Mr. Masked Marksman."

Ed said mildly, "You are really an unreasonable fellow, Bickert. I'm sure you'll never forgive me for this."

He wrenched Bickert's hand off the girl's arm, then gave him a hearty shove which sent him hurtling into the elevator cage to collide with the two detectives. Then Ed winked at Sammy.

Sammy returned the wink and slid the door shut, cooping the three detectives in the cage. Then he sent the elevator up. Ed saw the indicator go to five before it stopped. He grinned.

"Sammy is a good boy. I owe him another twenty for that!"

In the meantime he was propelling the girl swiftly out of the lobby and into the street. "We only have about a minute-and-a-half start on Bickert and his boyfriends," Ed told her. "They're on the way down already!"

THERE WAS a police squad car parked at the curb, right alongside the "No Parking" sign in front of the hotel. It was the car that Bickert had come in. Ed looked for a cab, saw one cruising toward the hotel entrance, and started to hail it. Just then someone said, "In there!"

He felt something hard jabbing into his back. Two men had come up on either side of him and the girl. One man was at his left, and it was he who was jabbing a gun into his ribs. The other man, on the girl's right, had hold of her arm, and he was poking a gun at her out of the pocket of his topcoat.

The man next to Ed jerked his head toward a limousine that had pulled up just behind the empty police squad car. He was short and skinny, and he had wide, bulging eyes, and buck teeth. There were hundreds of people passing, but no one noticed the concealed guns in the hands of Bulgy-eyes and his companion.

Grace Inness was staring at Bulgy-eyes. "You—you were in my brother's room talking to Lefty Mott. You killed Lefty!"

"Snap it up!" Bulgy-eyes snarled. "Or I'll let you have it, too—just as lieve!"

"Now isn't that nice!" said Ed. He swung suddenly to the left, his elbow jamming the gun out of alignment with his ribs. And he continued that motion, bringing his right fist all the way around to connect in a vicious *smack* to the side of Bulgy-eyes' head. Bulgy's gun exploded into the pavement, and he went cascading backward into a group of passersby, clawing to regain his balance.

Ed whirled back to the right, snaking the .45 out of his left-hand holster. But he was too late. The other man had hustled the girl across the pavement and into the waiting limousine. Just as Ed turned, the limousine's door slammed shut and it spurted away from the curb with wide-open accelerator. For an instant, Ed caught a glimpse of a face at the back window of the fleeing car—a long, thin face with black hair parted slickly in the middle. It was a face he knew.

"Sandoval!" he exclaimed, under his breath.

The limousine was out in traffic now. Another car came up behind it, and Ed couldn't shoot at the tires. The rest of Rick Sandoval's car, he knew, would be bulletproof. And then the limousine was gone from sight, turning the corner into the side street.

There was a shout behind Ed, and he swung around to see Sergeant Bickert and his two detectives erupting from the Longmont Hotel. They had seen Ed and started for him, but Bickert collided with Bulgy-eyes, who was just scrambling to his feet, picking up the gun he had dropped. A crowd of passersby was surging around, all trying to keep as far away as possible from the guns in Ed's hand and in that of Bulgy-eyes. And in their efforts to escape, they impeded the progress of Bickert's two sidekicks, who were trying to get to Ed Race.

Ed seized the opportunity to turn and run. He kept his revolver out and weaved through the crowd toward the Fiftieth Street subway kiosk. Men and women got out of his way, and he raced down the steps. A local train was roaring into the station, but Ed didn't make for it.

He ran past the cashier's booth to the other stairway at the south end of the station, and mounted the steps two at a time. They brought him up at the southwest corner of Fiftieth. He looked across the street and saw a crowd gathered in front of the other kiosk. They were looking down there, apparently after the detectives who had pursued him, and someone in the crowd shouted, "He got away on the train!"

Ed grinned sourly and turned away. He headed west along Fiftieth Street. He wasn't by any means out of trouble. Hansen and Bickert could easily pick him up tonight when he went on the stage at the Clyde.

He had stuck his chin out this time, for fair. There was no sense in it. A girl he had never seen before was in trouble. Her brother was involved in a murder. Rick Sandoval, New York's Number One Gambling Baron, was interested in it somehow. That was all Ed Race knew of the set-up. And with that little knowledge, he was in it up to his neck.

Thus far he was guilty of hiding the corpse of a murdered man, aiding a suspect to escape, assaulting a police officer, and creating a disturbance on a public street. Inspector Hansen would throw the book at him. And he had to face the music.

Ed Race was too well known to just pack up and run away. Besides, he would never do that. Somehow, he was convinced that the girl and her brother were the victims of some kind of elaborate plot on the part of Rick Sandoval. All he had to go on was the fact that he had seen Sandoval's face for an instant in the limousine. But when Hansen and Bickert picked him up tonight at the Clyde, he wouldn't be able to offer a word in his own defense.

He was halfway down the block when he discovered that someone had fallen into step alongside him, at his left. It was a man of about thirty-five, with sharply-chiseled features. He had a straight nose and thin lips, a stubborn chin, and brown hair which was thinning a little at the top. He had his hat in his hand in front of him, and he raised the hat a bit to show Ed the snout of a snub-nosed automatic underneath it. The automatic was pointing at Ed.

"Just keep walking!" he ordered grimly. "I want to talk to you."

ED RACE sighed. This was the third time within twenty minutes that a gun had been pointed at him. The fellow looked hard and coldly efficient, so Ed kept on walking. His hands swung free at his sides, ready for a lightning flash to one of his shoulder holsters.

"Go on and talk," he said.

"Where did they take my sister?" the man asked. "You fingered her for Rick Sandoval to grab. Well, you better cough up the dope. I want to know where Sandoval took her. In case you don't tell me quick, I'll give you a nice piece of lead in the stomach. And you know lead can't be digested."

He spoke coolly, but Ed could see a deep burning desperation in his eyes.

"You're Jack Inness," he said.

Inness's lips curled. "Maybe you didn't know it! Don't stall. Where did Sandoval take Grace?"

They were walking down the street just like two acquaintances conversing amiably. None of the passersby gave them a glance. But the hat in Inness' hand came up a little, and the muzzle of the automatic centered on Ed's stomach.

"You sap," Ed told him. "I was trying to help your sister. She found a dead body in your room, and she dragged it out into the hall. The police came along, and I helped her get the body into my room just in time. Then I took her downstairs. Sandoval was waiting in the limousine, and they grabbed her."

Inness' eyes widened. "A dead body! Who?"

"Lefty Mott."

Inness cursed under his breath. "Lefty was my trigger man. They got him. And they figured to frame me for it!"

Ed Race looked disgusted and puzzled. "*Your* trigger man! My God, what is this? First a seventeen-year-old girl tries to convince me that she's a gun moll. Then some muggs of Sandoval's try to convince me they're tough guys. Then *you* come along and try to tell me you're a big shot, with a trigger-man of your own. If this is a comedy of some kind, I know one guy that isn't enjoying it—Lefty Mott. And you can't be such a big shot. Because I never heard of anyone named Inness in the rackets."

Inness sighed, took the gun from under the hat and thrust it in his pocket. "I guess you're on the up-and-up," he said. "Maybe you never heard the name Inness. I didn't use it. But you've heard of 'Gentleman Jack' English?"

Ed nodded. A sudden gleam of understanding came into his eyes. "I should have known. You used to run the gambling racket in this town. Then the Federal Government caught up with you on income-tax evasion, and you went to Atlanta for three years. You were paroled just a few weeks ago."

"That's right. I used the name of English instead of Inness, because I didn't want my sister Gracie mixed up in the rackets," was the reply. "Gracie thinks I've been traveling in South America for the past three years. When I wrote her that I was back in New York, she came here from school to meet me. I didn't want her around, because I knew there was going to be trouble with Sandoval. Rick Sandoval"—Inness's lips twisted—"took over the racket while I was away. The mob went with him. Lefty Mott was the only one that stuck with me. It was Lefty that sent my sister Grace the letters and money from South America during the three years I was in the pen."

"I see," Ed said slowly. "And Sandoval's crowd killed Lefty Mott in your room, so the police would arrest you for it. Even if you aren't convicted, it'll break your parole and automatically send you back to the pen. And Sandoval will still have a clear field!"

Gentleman Jack English nodded bitterly. "When Grace showed up in New York, I acted like a sap and took a room for her right next to my own. I forgot that Sandoval had seen her picture lots of times in the old days, and would recognize her. She doesn't even know that her brother is Gentleman Jack English. I've kept her in a convent school all these years."

"Something tells me," Ed said dryly, "that the girls in that school smuggled in a few detective stories on the side. She knew a lot about gun molls and burning bodies in incinerators—just the kind of stuff they get in some books."

"I don't understand what Sandoval wanted to snatch Grace for," Jack English said. "He had me framed okay without that—"

"I'll tell you why," Ed said with a harsh note creeping into his voice. "Grace got a glimpse of the murderer!"

Gentleman Jack stopped short in his tracks. All the color drained from his face. "Then they'll kill her!" he said, very low. "They'll surely never let her live!"

"If they kill an innocent little kid like Grace—"

Gentleman Jack Inness uttered a hoarse, tortured laugh. "You don't know Sandoval. He's running the rackets worse than I ever ran them. He'll stick Grace's feet in a slab of concrete and drop her in the river!" There was a hot, mad light in his eyes. "God!" he muttered. "All the things I used to do are coming back at me now. That boathouse I used to have on the Hudson, at Sixty-eighth Street—Sandoval's still using it. God help me, Race—I've done plenty of bad things in my time in that boathouse. And now"—there was a sob in his voice—"it's my own sister's turn!"

He went to the curb, and waved wildly to a cruising cab.

Ed Race put a hand on his arm. "What are you going to do, Inness?"

Gentleman Jack's teeth showed in a snarl. "There's an alarm out for me for the murder of Lefty Mott. I can't ask the cops to help on this. I'm going up to that boathouse and take it apart myself!"

He jumped into the cab, yelled to the driver: "Foot of West Sixty-eighth Street!"

Ed Race exclaimed, "Look here, Inness, I'm going with you—"

But Gentleman Jack slammed the door shut in his face. "Nothing doing, Race. Stay out of this. It's my headache."

The cab spurted away from the curb.

And just then, a radio patrol car came cruising past.

ED RACE saw it all from where he stood at the curb. The radio car contained a sergeant and a driver. Ed saw the sergeant stare into the cab where Inness was sitting. He heard the sergeant exclaim, *"There's Gentleman Jack!"*

The driver of the police car swung in to cut off the taxicab.

Gentleman Jack opened the door of the car, leaped out and started to run.

The sergeant in the radio car deliberately raised his gun and fired once.

Gentleman Jack sprawled headlong on his face, with blood spurting from a wound in his back just over the heart.

Ed Race cursed softly to himself as he ran over to where Inness was lying on his face. The sergeant had also reached Gentleman Jack, and Ed helped him turn the dying man over on his back.

Gentleman Jack groaned. His lips were flecked with blood. He knew he was dying. His eyes swept past the sergeant and locked with the staring eyes of Ed Race.

"I got—what was coming to me. But—Gracie—for God's sake, don't let her get it, too…."

Ed Race gulped. He pressed Gentleman Jack's hand, and nodded an unspoken promise.

Inness smiled. He closed his eyes. His head dropped back into the sergeant's arms. He was dead.

The sergeant looked at Ed. "What the hell was he talking about?"

Ed shrugged. "I wouldn't know. I'm just a passerby."

A crowd was pressing close about them. Ed slid out inconspicuously to the edge of the crowd and moved over to the taxicab out of which Inness had jumped. His eyes were bleak. "Foot of West Sixty-eighth Street!" he said to the driver.

AS THE cab pulled away, Ed saw the police sergeant getting up from beside the dead body of Gentleman Jack Inness, and staring after him. The sergeant was just realizing that Ed Race had been more than an innocent bystander, that he must in some way have been connected with Inness. Several bystanders had heard Ed's order to the cab driver, and Ed knew that the police would not be far behind him.

As the cab swung west, Ed stared ahead grimly. His word was given—to a dead man. And even if he had not promised, the thought of innocent little Gracie Inness sinking helplessly to the bottom of the river with her feet buried in a slab of concrete would have impelled him to go ahead. He knew that what he had to do, he must do alone. For at this moment he could not call upon the police. Inspector Hansen or Sergeant Bickert would clap him in jail first, and question him.

To send the police on a raid of the 68th Street boathouse would be equivalent to signing Grace Inness's death warrant. For Rick Sandoval would be sure to see to it that she was the first to die. Sandoval and his gang could not afford to have her remain alive to identify the killer of Lefty Mott.

At 67th Street and Twelfth Avenue, Ed Race dismissed his

cab and walked a block north. He spotted the boathouse at once. It was a low, well-kept structure jutting out into the river. A sign across the door read,

SANDOVAL BOAT CLUB

Jack Inness had once owned all that property. Ed recalled hearing through underground rumor that, when Inness went to jail, he had deeded all his holdings to Sandoval to administer for him. And Sandoval had immediately proceeded to double-cross his former chief and to use all this property as his own.

This same boat club had figured in the death of many a man who in the past had dared to defy the underworld rule of Gentleman Jack English.

Ed Race came to a stop directly across the street from the Boat Club. There was a single dim light at the side of the building, and he could see that a long, sleek cabin-cruiser was tied up at the dock, alongside the low building.

Ed Race's eyes were bleak as he crossed the street. His hands swung low at his sides. As he reached the entrance of the building, a dark figure separated itself from the shadows and barred the door.

"Hello, Butch," said Ed. The blood raced in his veins. Now he was sure that Gentleman Jack had not been mistaken. This must be where they had taken Grace Inness, otherwise why would Butch Halsey, Sandoval's personal bodyguard, be on watch here?

Butch Halsey had his hand in his coat pocket. "What you doin' here—Race?"

Ed smiled thinly. "Just going in to see Rick Sandoval," he said.

"Sandoval ain't here," Butch told him.

"I'll see for myself, thank you."

Ed started to go in, and Butch barred the way. "Scram," he said. His hand came out of his pocket with a wicked little gunmetal automatic.

But he had no chance against Ed Race, whose exhibitions of lightning draws nightly amazed the audiences at the Clyde Theater. Ed's right hand streaked in almost imperceptible motion, and somehow as if by magic, a huge, long-barreled .45 was coming down in a short, wicked arc. The barrel smashed against Butch's wrist, and he dropped the automatic.

Ed was smiling casually, but there was a deadly glint in his eyes.

"Now," he said softly, "turn around and open that door and go in."

Butch gulped. He was no longer the tough gangster bodyguard. He had no guts to buck a lightning draw like Ed's. "The—the door is locked," he said, gulping again.

Ed's eyes rested on a bell alongside the door. "All right. There must be a signal to get the door open. Ring that bell properly."

BUTCH HESITATED for the space of ten seconds. He looked into Ed's eyes, and what he saw there made up his mind for him. Slowly he turned around and put his thumb on the bell button. He pressed it twice, then stopped, and pressed it three times swiftly again. Almost at once, a buzzer sounded. Butch pushed the door open. Ed took out one of his guns and nudged him in the back. Butch understood, and he led the way down the dark hallway. There was a light at the far end of the building, and Ed urged the husky bodyguard ahead of him toward that light. They could hear voices inside. Someone called out, "Hurry up, Butch. Give us a hand with this!"

Ed and Butch reached the entrance to the room at the rear. The far end of the room had sliding doors which opened onto the pier. Three men were standing around the figure of Grace Inness. For a moment, as Ed looked at that tableau, it seemed to him that little Grace Inness was taller than any of the three men.

Grace Inness was not standing on the floor. Her feet were resting in a slab of concrete about three feet square and three feet high. They were buried up to the ankles in the concrete. Rick Sandoval and two of his men were pushing the heavy slab out onto the pier. It was evidently their intention to get their victim onto the cabin-cruiser, take her out into the center of the river, and drop her over.

The gaunt face of Sandoval looked up at Butch, who was in the doorway in front of Ed Race.

"Come on, Butch," he called. "You have the shoulders for this."

And then Sandoval saw Ed Race behind the big bodyguard. He uttered a shout of warning to the other two men and dropped to the floor. A gun came into his hand. The other two men went to their knees behind the suddenly huddled figure of Grace Inness. Butch Halsey squealed as shots from their three guns came thundering at the doorway. They weren't worried about Butch.

Halsey took the first fusillade in his chest and fell forward, leaving Ed alone.

Grace Inness was staring in Ed s direction, unable to move out of the concrete bed in which she had been encased. She was a perfect shield for Sandoval and the two gunmen. That is, she *would* have made a perfect shield against anyone except The Masked Marksman.

Ed Race stood spraddle-legged.

The two hair-trigger .45 caliber revolvers were in his hands, bucking and roaring as he fired carefully.

His first shot chipped an edge off the concrete block, sending the splinters into the eyes of one of the gunmen. The man dropped his gun and screamed.

Sandoval and the remaining thug kept on shooting. But they were not aiming. They were just triggering their guns in blind fear. Both of them knew who Ed Race was. They had seen The Masked Marksman on the stage.

They knew that if Ed could see only an inch of their bodies, he could hit that inch. So they squirmed close to the ground, pressing together behind the three-foot concrete slab, seeking all the protection they could. And from that position, their shooting was none too certain.

Ed saw a shoulder and fired once, hitting it. The gunman with Sandoval squealed and fell flat on the ground. Sandoval cursed and raised his gun, pointing directly up at Grace Inness.

"Stop shooting, Race," he yelled, "or I'll kill the girl!"

Ed Race laughed harshly. All he could see of Sandoval to shoot at was the barrel of his gun, jutting up from behind the concrete slab and pointing at Grace. That barrel was no wider than a candle.

The two slugs whined through the air, converging upon that tiny target. The gun was smashed from Sandoval's hand and went spinning across the floor. Sandoval cursed and rolled over. In his left hand he seized the gun dropped by one of his men. But Ed Race had already leaped across the room toward the slab. He pulled the trigger of his right-hand gun four times in quick succession. The four slugs smashed Sandoval's right wrist.

"Don't—shoot anymore!" he begged.

Ed's eyes glinted with a bleak light.

Abruptly, the sound of a police siren cut through the air outside, accompanied by the screaming of tires on pavement. In a moment, uniformed men flooded into the building, headed by Hansen.

Ed Race holstered his guns. "You can arrest me now, if you want to, Hansen," he said dryly. "But I think you've got bigger fish for your net!"

He turned, just in time to catch the slumping body of Grace Inness as she fell.

"By God," Inspector Hansen exclaimed, "what's been going on here, Race?"

"Nothing much," said Ed. "Except that you've got Rick Sandoval cold for attempted murder. And when Grace Inness comes out of her fainting spell, she can identify the murderer of Lefty Mott. Now, you might get some pick-axes and chip this concrete off her feet."

Hansen swore softly. He motioned to his men to find axes. Then he looked at Ed. "You shot it out with this mob?"

Ed nodded. "I had to do the job myself. You wouldn't have given me a chance to explain."

Inspector Hansen grunted. "Frankly, Race, I don't like you. But I got to give the devil his due. You did a nice piece of work."

"Thanks," said Ed, starting for the door. "I'll be down at headquarters later to sign a statement. In the meantime, take good care of Gracie. I'm going to see that she gets a good start in life—the kind her brother would have liked to see her get."

"Hey, wait a minute!" Hansen yelled. "Where are you going?"

"It's one o'clock," Ed called back from the doorway. "I have a curtain call at the Clyde at one-ten—to put on an exhibition of *real* shooting!"

HEADLINER FROM HELL

ON FORTY-EIGHTH STREET, between Seventh Avenue and Eighth, stood a blind man—a cane in one hand, hat in the other. His smoked glasses were very large, and covered a considerable part of his face.

Ed Race, walking west from the Clyde Theater, saw the blind man, and started to fumble a quarter out of his pocket. Ed was a pushover for every panhandler on the Main Stem. But he made ample money to afford the countless dimes and quarters he handed out every day. On the marquee of the Clyde Theater his name showed in electric lights:

SPECIAL RETURN ENGAGEMENT
THE MASKED MARKSMAN
THE MAN WHO CAN MAKE GUNS TALK!

It is quite possible that, if the blind man had known that Ed Race was the Masked Marksman, he would have chosen some other post tonight. For it appeared that this particular blind man wasn't really looking for any handouts. He seemed nervous, anxious merely to be left alone.

Though he couldn't have seen Ed's hand with the quarter in it, he actually made an involuntary motion with his hat in such a way that the coin would drop into it quickly. And he muttered a hurried "Thanks," before the quarter hit the hat.

Now many blind men have a feeling about these things which amounts to unerring instinct. Ed knew that the blind news dealer around the corner from the Clyde could tell by the rustle of paper just which magazine a customer was picking up. But it was a little too much to expect that a man without the use of his eyes could catch a coin in his hat from the air.

Ed might not have noticed it if he had not trained himself from necessity to keep all senses constantly alert. He didn't mind being rooked out of a quarter by a bogus blind man, because he'd have given a handout to anyone. But he was interested.

He looked sharply at the mendicant. "You know," he said, "I don't think I've seen you around here before. You new on this street?"

"Yeah," said the blind man. "I'm new. Well, so long, mister. I'll be seein' you again—I mean—stop by again."

Ed laughed. "Just a little slip of the tongue, eh? I don't think you're blind at all."

He was startled by the sudden transformation in the man. A stream of vile language burst from the fellow. He dropped the hat, and his hand darted to his shoulder, under his coat. It came out with a gun. Through the smoked glasses, the fellow's eyes were now visible, glaring at Ed.

This was right up Ed Race's alley. He was a little bewildered that a phony beggar should pull a gun. But his muscles reacted with the trained split-second efficiency required of them on the stage. In his vaudeville act he daily brought the audiences to the edge of their seats with the almost uncanny speed of his draw. One of his numbers consisted of juggling six Ping-Pong

Ed's guns began to bark!

balls in the air. He would get them into play, send them high up, then stand at ease as they descended. Just as the audience thought that the balls were surely going to hit the floor, two heavy .45 caliber hair-trigger revolvers appeared in Ed's hands.

Each gun would blast three times—and nothing remained of the six Ping-Pong balls.

So, the bogus blind-man was shocked when he got his gun out of the shoulder holster—only to have the barrel of a huge .45 smack down on his wrist. Ed's .45 seemed to have come from nowhere....

That quick draw and downward slash with the revolver had been timed so beautifully—executed with such lightning speed—that no one passing in the street could have seen it. And then, with equal speed, the revolver slid back into Ed Race's shoulder clip.

Ed grinned down into the bewildered face of the blind man, who stared stupidly from his numb wrist to the automatic lying on the sidewalk.

Abruptly, a terrific fright seemed to grip the blind man. He ripped off the smoked glasses, dropped them—discarded the cane and hat. Then he turned and streaked like a rabbit for the corner.

ED DIDN'T bother to halt the fleeing man. He only laughed. He stooped, picked up the other's automatic, put it in his pocket. Then he gathered up the hat, cane and glasses. He tried on the glasses, to discover how much the faker had been able to see through them. For an instant he was wearing the glasses—holding the hat and cane just as the faker had done.

And in that instant a limousine pulled to a stop at the curb. It slid up smoothly.

There was no chauffeur in it. A girl with richly tinted auburn hair and violet eyes was at the wheel. She left the motor running, opened the door—got out quickly. She had a package in her hand and came straight over to Ed. She said nothing, just looked at him queerly, with a terrible intensity in her violet eyes, and a little twitching of her sensitive lips. Then she dropped the package in the hat he was holding, and hurried back into the car.

She closed the door with a bang, threw a quick glance at him. Then she said through clenched teeth, "If you don't play fair, I swear I'll follow you to the ends of the earth!"

A moment later, gears clashed and the car leaped away.

Ed started to call after her, but she was already too far away to hear. All he could do was to note the license number—ES-9. Then the limousine turned the corner into Seventh Avenue.

Ed scratched his head. He put the cane under his arm, took the package out of the hat, and examined it. It was wrapped in white figured paper like the stuff they put on candy boxes, and it was tied with red string. He pulled at one corner of the wrapper, uncovered the contents. Then he whistled. The package was about four inches thick, and full of hundred-dollar bills. There were between three and four hundred bills in the package—which meant that it contained between thirty and forty thousand dollars.

"A nice wad for a lady to drop into a blind beggar's hat!" Ed said out loud.

"That's right, my friend!" someone said behind him. "Not a bad wad at all!"

Ed Race swung around. There was a narrow alley between two buildings, in front of which the bogus blind beggar had been standing. In this alley now stood two men. Handkerchiefs covered the lower part of their faces, so that only the eyes were visible under the hat-brim. Both were about the same height, but one was more broadly built than the other. Each held a black, large-calibered automatic—pointed at Ed's stomach.

The heavier of the two men was the one who had spoken. He said, "I'll trouble you, my friend, to throw that package over here."

"No trouble at all," said Ed.

He flipped the package toward them with his left hand. The man who had spoken reached to catch it. Momentarily, he was slightly in front of his partner. For the split fraction of an instant, the eyes of neither were on Ed Race. They did not see that his hand had continued its motion after throwing the package. His right hand moved up at the same time, and both hands crossed over his chest. Two revolvers were now in them.

The man who had caught the package saw the gleam of metal, and uttered a quick cry. The cry choked off in his throat as the barrel of Ed's gun smashed against his temple. He dropped like a log, and the package of money fell to the ground.

The other man gasped with fright when he saw the two huge guns Ed held. He didn't try to shoot. He turned and scampered down the alley, disappearing into the shadows.

Ed's first instinct was to follow. Then he shrugged, stooped and picked up the money. He stuffed the package into his pocket, and knelt beside the unconscious masked man. He pulled off the handkerchief, and frowned. The man's face was unfamiliar.

He heard heavy footsteps on the sidewalk, and turned around to see Pat Garrity, the cop on the beat.

"Hello, Mr. Race," said the cop. "What goes on—?"

"This fellow tried to hold me up," Ed told him. "His pal got away, but I beaned this one." Some queer instinct made Ed refrain from mentioning the package of money. It was not that he wanted it for himself. He had plenty. But the circumstances of his receiving it had been so unusual that he wanted a chance to look into this business. That girl with the violet eyes certainly had wanted to keep the transaction a secret. There must be some potent reason for her actions. He wanted to find out more about her—without getting her in trouble.

"Call the wagon and take this egg to the precinct house, Pat," he said. "I'll be around in an hour. I've got something to attend to."

Pat looked at him and scratched his head. "I guess it's okay, Mr. Race. Go ahead."

IT WASN'T exactly an infraction of the rules for a cop to let a complaining witness leave without signing a complaint at the station house. But usually they hang on to a witness till they have everything down in black and white. In Ed's case it was different.

Garrity knew that Ed was a personal friend of Inspector MacSpain, the commander of detectives for the Borough of Manhattan. Ed had worked with the police closely many times in the past. His uncanny ability with guns, plus a degree of nervous energy which demanded action and excitement all the time, had compelled Ed Race to seek an avocation in addition to his regular job. That avocation was criminology. He had licenses to operate as a private detective in a dozen states. And the name of Ed Race was as much detested in the rackets as the name of the Masked Marksman was applauded by theater audiences.

So Pat Garrity felt no qualms when Ed nodded to him and hurried up the street with the package containing forty thousand dollars in his pocket.

Ed went no farther than the corner drugstore on Eighth Avenue, where he slipped into a 'phone booth and called the night emergency number of the New York State Motor Vehicle Bureau. This office is kept open twenty-four hours a day for the purpose of aiding the police in checking on stolen cars and hit-and-run drivers.

"Inspector MacSpain's office calling," he said when he got the connection. "I want the name and address of the owner of a limousine bearing the license number, ES-nine."

"We will call you back, Inspector," said the operator.

Ed grimaced, and hung up. He inserted another nickel, and called the Borough Detective Commander's office, in the Tenth Precinct Station House on Twentieth Street.

"Mac!" he said, when he got the Inspector. "There's a call coming in for you from the Motor Vehicle Bureau. I used your name. Get the information while I hold this wire!"

"All right, Eddie," said MacSpain. "But where's the fire? Are you into something up to your neck? I never saw anyone like you for attracting trouble. You're a magnet."

"I've got something on my hands, Mac, but I don't know what it adds up to, yet. Don't ask me to tell you too much. There's some of it you shouldn't know—officially. But it has to do with blind beggars who can see, and dames who hand out forty grand for a cup of coffee. And by the way, maybe you should take a run up to the West Forty-Seventh Street Precinct. There's a bird in there who's being held for attempted robbery—of me."

MacSpain whistled. "The sap. I'll go over and talk to him—wait—here's your dope from the M.V.B. Hold on."

In a moment he was back on the wire. "Here you are, Eddie. The car belongs to no less a personage than—Elspeth Sinclair, Groton Heights Apartments, Central Park South. That's the Four Hundred, Eddie. Old Warren Sinclair owns half the cattle in the Argentine. Elspeth's his daughter, and he has a son a couple of years younger than her, named Austin. Then there's a cousin named Courtney Sinclair. They have nine cars in the family, all with license plates according to their initials. Old Warren is the meanest man on earth. The cop on his beat gets a dollar for Christmas. And he gives his two kids and their cousin all the luxuries they can use—but no spending money in cash. They say Elspeth has to borrow fifteen cents if she's out alone and wants to buy a pack of butts!"

"That's funny," Ed told him. "She must have been saving her cigarette money a long time—with interest, so it could grow to forty grand!"

"What's that—?"

"Not now, Mac. I'm in a hurry. Mucho hurry. Go up and see that ginzo at the Forty-Seventh Street Precinct. I'll call you there and give you the low-down!"

He hung up and went out quickly. There was a cab at the curb, and he got into it.

"Central Park South," he said.

THE GROTON HEIGHTS APARTMENTS was a pretty tall building, with a gorgeous view of Central Park, two doormen, and a couple of extra uniformed flunkeys who were there apparently just to give the tenants the idea that they were getting their money's worth.

One of the doormen held the cab door open. Ed told the driver to wait, and started to go in. But the other doorman stopped him, courteously but very firmly.

"May I have your name, sir?" he asked. "And the name of the person you are calling on? I will announce you on the 'phone."

"I want to see Miss Elspeth Sinclair," Ed told him. "The name is Race."

"Thank you, sir. Have you an appointment, sir?"

"No. Tell her it's the man she met on Forty-Eighth Street tonight."

The doorman raised his eyebrows. He went to the 'phone in the foyer, plugged it in. But just then the elevator came down to the ground floor and the door slid open—and Ed saw the violet-eyed girl come out upon the arm of a tall, well-knit man of about forty. Both were in evening clothes.

Ed's eyes narrowed. He knew that man. On the Main Stem they called him Pug Lester, and he was known as the greatest crook gambler in town. He owned the Villa Lester, just across the river, where you could bet five thousand dollars on a number at the roulette wheel, or ten thousand dollars on the turn of a card at blackjack. He also owned three or four similar places in New York, but none were half as swanky as the one across the river. Pug Lester's society name was Percival Wayland Lester.

His family was an old and respected one, but Pug Lester had certainly become a black sheep. There were quite a few unsolved killings in recent years, which the police would have liked to pin on him. But his money and his influence always managed to protect the thugs in his employ. So far nobody had ever got anything on him. As usual with a dashing, handsome chap like Lester, he was the darling of the younger set in the most fashionable circles.

To Ed Race, Elspeth Sinclair looked even more beautiful than when she had put the package in his hat.

The doorman came over and whispered to her, indicating Ed with a nod. Pug Lester frowned. Elspeth Sinclair looked at Ed, and there was nothing in her face to show that she recognized him. Those goggles hadn't been much of a disguise, and his build and his fair hair should have been enough to recall him to her. But she shook her head with a slight frown of annoyance, and Ed heard her say, "I'm sorry, but I don't know the gentleman. Please see that I am not annoyed now."

The doorman bowed, and came over to Ed. He was no longer courteous. "I'm sorry. But you'll have to leave. Miss Sinclair does not know you—"

Ed brushed the man aside, and stepped across the lobby to where she stood with Pug Lester.

Lester's face darkened and he said, "Wait here, Elspeth. I'll get rid of the fellow."

Ed disregarded him. "I've got to talk to you, Miss Sinclair," he said. "I have something to return to you—something that belongs to you."

Her eyes were cold, her lips set tightly. "I am not interested. Please leave."

"Surely, Miss Sinclair, you remember seeing me tonight," Ed said. "You put something in my hat."

She raised her eyebrows. "Something in your hat? You are mad. What would I put something in your hat for?"

"I don't know," Ed said. "But it was a lot of money. Forty thousand dollars. Don't you want it back?"

Elspeth Sinclair turned to Pug Lester. "I am afraid this man is deranged, Perk. Please—Take me out!"

Lester said, "Okay." He glared at Ed. "You heard what the lady said. She never saw you before. Now are you going to get out of here, or do we call the police?"

Ed shrugged. "I'll go—and thanks for the forty thousand, Miss Sinclair. If you should want it back—my name is Race. I live at the Longmont Hotel—Room Seven-Sixteen."

He turned on his heel and marched out of the lobby. His ears were red. He couldn't understand the girl's denials—unless she was trying to hide something from Pug Lester. In that case she could have given Ed some signal, some sign that she really did know him. But she had been as cold and uncompromising as a marble statue in a January wind.

Outside, Ed saw the limousine with the ES-9 license plate, parked up ahead of his cab. His eyes flickered with an idea, He went over to his driver, but did not get into the taxi.

"Here's twenty bucks," he said, handing the man a bill. "Follow the girl and the man who are coming out of here. Call me at the Longmont Hotel, Trafalgar Two-four-eight-four-eight, and ask for Edward Race. Report where they go. Keep with them all night if you have to. Do this job right, and there's fifty dollars more in it for you."

The driver grinned. "For that kind of money, Mister Race, I'll follow them to China."

Ed said slowly, "The man is Pug Lester. Does that make a difference?"

The driver's face darkened. "Yeah—this much difference: I had a kid brother who got knocked off once by one of Lester's hoods. I'd do this job for nothing, Mister Race!"

Ed nodded. He got in the cab, and the driver pulled away, turned the corner. Ed hopped out, and the cabby backed around so as to get a view of the entrance of the Groton Heights Apartments. Two minutes later he nodded to Ed and started off across Central Park South on the tail of the limousine. Ed saw that Elspeth Sinclair was driving, and Pug Lester was sitting beside her.

ED FINGERED the package of money in his coat pocket, then hailed another cab and went to the Longmont Hotel. As he got into his room, the 'phone was ringing. It was Inspector MacSpain, calling from the West Forty-Seventh Street Station House.

"What the hell kind of hornet's nest have *you* been stirring up, Eddie?" he demanded.

"Why?"

"I've just talked to the chap that Pat Garrity brought in here for attempting to rob you. He claims that *you* robbed *him.* He says you knocked him out and took forty thousand dollars from his pocket."

"That's a nice story," Ed laughed. "But he ought to think of a better one. I bet he has a record."

"No," said MacSpain, "he hasn't got a record. In fact, he's pretty clean. You'll see what I mean when I tell you who he is."

"All right, all right, I'll bite!" Ed barked. "Who is he?"

"His name," MacSpain said slowly, "is Courtney Sinclair. He's Elspeth Sinclair's cousin!"

"Well I'll be damned!" said Ed.

"You'll be worse than damned, Eddie," MacSpain told him. "You'll be jugged. He's swearing out a warrant for *your* arrest on a charge of robbery. And it's his word against yours. Better come down here and surrender yourself, or they'll be coming for you. And I can't stop it, Eddie. It's the law!"

"Okay," Ed said wearily. "See if you can hold up the warrant for about an hour. I'll be down then. In the meantime, I'll see what I can do about putting this jigsaw together. I'm going to call Elspeth's father—old Warren Sinclair—and see if I can pump anything out of him."

He hung up, and immediately jiggled the hook for the operator at the switchboard downstairs. "Get me the home of Mr. Warren Sinclair, at the Groton Heights Apartments, on Central Park South."

He heard the dial tone, and then a man's pompous voice answered, "This is the residence of Mr. Warren Sinclair. Mr. Sinclair's secretary speaking."

"I wish to talk to Mr. Warren Sinclair personally," Ed said.

"Who is calling, please?"

"J.P. Morgan," Ed told him.

"Ah, one moment, Mr. Morgan. I shall call Mr. Sinclair at once!"

There was a short wait, and Ed heard a startled ejaculation over the 'phone. Then, "Mr. Morgan, sir! A terrible thing has happened. Mr. Sinclair has been murdered!"

"How?" Ed rapped.

"Shot, sir. There—there's a bullet hole in his head. I… it's *awful,* sir!"

"All right. Hang up and ring the police," Ed said. "Tell them to report this to Inspector MacSpain personally. Have you got it?"

Ed put down the 'phone. And just as he did so, some one rapped heavily on the door.

Ed frowned. He walked over, pulled the door open—and two men came barging into the room with guns in their hands. One was the bogus blind beggar from Forty-Eighth Street. The other was a hard-eyed killer with cold, reptilian eyes.

The beggar waved his gun, said to his companion, "That's the guy, Pelley. That's the guy got the dough! Pug figured it right!"

Pelley grinned thinly. He kept his gun on Ed's stomach. "Okay, pal," he said, thin-lipped. "You got forty grand belonging to a friend of mine. Hand it over."

Ed rocked back on his heels, eying the two men, and not smiling at all.

"Pug Lester sent you?" he asked harshly.

"Never mind who sent us!" Pelley snarled. "Hand over the dough."

"How do I know it belongs to Pug?"

"You don't have to know nothing. See this?" He raised the muzzle of the gun just a little. "*This* is all you got to worry about."

"Is that the same gun that killed old Warren Sinclair?" Ed asked softly.

Pelley stiffened. His eyes became little pinpoints of murderous venom. His voice was soft and silky. "I'm afraid you know too much for your health, mister." He looked sideways at the bogus blind man, who had been swiftly fanning the room, looking in bureau drawers and under the mattress. "Did you find the dough yet, Luke?"

"Nah!" said Luke. "It ain't in the room. He must still have it in his pocket."

Pelley's eyes were bright. He extended his left hand, alongside of the gun in his right. "Give!" he said to Ed.

Ed shrugged. "Well, if that's the way you feel about it—" His hand went up to the breast pocket of his coat.

"Look out!" yelled Luke. "He's got a gun there—!"

But the warning was too late.

Ed Race's body was already in motion. Many an audience in the vaudeville theaters from coast to coast had watched with bulging eyes while the Masked Marksman did his double-somersault number—where he juggled six of those heavy .45 caliber revolvers, did a double back-flip, then came to his feet to catch the guns and shoot out the flames of a row of candles thirty feet across the stage.

Mr. Pelley and Mr. Luke now were privileged to witness the same exhibition of swiftly blinding skill—but instead of paying for their tickets with money, they paid with blood.

Ed's first shot as he came to his feet out of the somersault, blended with the bark of Pelley's gun. Only the deep-toned roar of the heavy .45 almost drowned it out. Pelley had never seen a victim who moved so swiftly and bafflingly. His bullet scorched the air where Ed had been standing before the somersault, dug into the wall harmlessly. Ed's slug smashed into Pelley's shoulder with the weight of a ton of bricks, and sent him crashing into the wall. Ed had purposely fired at his shoulder, because he wanted to keep the tough gunman alive. He wanted a confession from Pelley.

He did not even look to see where he had hit the cold-eyed gunman. He never looked, because his slugs always went where he sent them. He pivoted on one heel and faced Luke just as the bogus blind man brought his gun around to bear on Ed. Ed stepped in swiftly, and for the second time that night he smacked the blind man. This time though, he brought the muzzle of his gun sharply up against the tip of Luke's jaw, and Luke collapsed like a marionette whose string has broken.

Ed got a pair of handcuffs from his trunk, and cuffed the two men together, passing the links through the bedpost.

"That ought to hold you for a little while!" he said grimly.

He started for the door, and the 'phone rang. He scooped it up impatiently, said, "Hello."

"Hey, Mister Race. This is Blivens—you know, the cab driver. I been stickin' to Pug Lester and that dame—"

"Where are they now?" Ed asked tensely.

"It's screwy, Mister Race, and I don't get it at all," the cabby said. "They went to one of Pug Lester's joints—the Casa Midnight, on Fifty-Seventh Street. The girl sat down at a table, and Lester went in his office in the back. Then a guy comes and sits down and talks to the dame for a couple minutes, and scrams. The dame gets white, and excited, kind of. I seen it all from the checkroom. She gets up and goes and knocks on Lester's door, and he opens it and she tells him something. Then she says goodbye to him and comes tearin' out and gets in her car. So I figure as long as Lester is in his office, I'll tail her. She drives like a bat out of hell across to Tenth Avenue, and goes in a warehouse—the old Abercombie Warehouse, which ain't been used in five years. She don't have no trouble opening the door and getting in."

"The Abercombie Warehouse!" Ed exclaimed. "That used to be a paint company. Is she there now?"

"Wait, Mister Race. You ain't heard it all yet. I figure she will be out right away again, so I park down the middle of next block, with my lights out. And who do you suppose comes along?"

"Pug Lester!"

"You smacked the nail on the head, Mister Race. Pug Lester and three of his gorillas. They park around the corner, an' go in. So I figure it's time to 'phone you—"

"You bet it is!" Ed shouted. "I'll be right over there. You put another nickel in the 'phone and call the cops. Tell them to shoot a radio car over there right away. And also tell Inspector

MacSpain to come to my room at the Longmont and pick up two men!"

HE SWIFTLY gathered up the guns of Luke and Pelley, who were still unconscious. Pelley was bleeding, but Ed didn't even stop to help him. His eyes were bleak. He was beginning to understand the set-up.

He wrapped the guns carefully in handkerchiefs so as not to destroy the fingerprints, and put them in his pocket with the forty-thousand dollar package. Then he went out and locked the door.

He got a cab downstairs, said, "Shoot across to Tenth Avenue—and *don't* stop for lights. Just blow your horn and keep going. I'll cover you for everything!"

The cabby was a regular at the hack stand in front of the Longmont, and knew Ed. He simply nodded, sent the taxi ahead, and kept his elbow on the horn all the time. How he managed to avoid smash-ups all the way over, only the gods of the taxi drivers know. But he got to the Abercombie Warehouse in two minutes and twenty-seven seconds. On the way over, Ed heard the clang of fire engines back near Broadway, and the wail of police sirens. There must be a big fire somewhere along the Main Stem, he thought. But he thrust it from his mind when he got to the warehouse.

Blivens, his cabby-detective, was waiting across the street. But there was no police car.

"Did you 'phone the cops like I told you?" Ed asked.

Blivens nodded. "A radio car ought to be here any minute—"

"Any minute may be too late!" Ed rapped. "I'm going in there now. When the cops come, send them after me!"

He ran across the street, and leaped up to the old loading platform in front of the decrepit warehouse. There was a small door alongside the big loading doors, which were closed. But the small one opened under his hand, and he stepped inside. It was pitch dark, but Ed caught a glimmer of light at the rear. He made his way toward it, ears attuned to catch the first sounds of arriving police outside. He could hear no siren, however.

The smell of creosote was strong in his nostrils. Though this warehouse had not been used in years, the paint odors still lingered. No doubt the place was impregnated with the stuff.

As he approached the rear, he saw that the source of light was the small, glassed-in office at the back. It was coming from a candle inside the office. The glass panel of the office door was broken, and Ed could see the figures of two men moving about in there, but he couldn't see Elspeth.

He moved soundlessly, until within ten feet of the office. The two men were talking in low tones. He heard Pug Lester say, "Got to get this through quick, Sykes. Snap it up!"

Ed stiffened. He heard a faint sound behind him, and then a gun jabbed him in the back. "All right, wise guy. Keep going."

Ed said, "Hell! What a sucker I am. I forgot there were three of you!"

"Sucker is the word!" muttered his captor, then raised his voice. "Look what I picked outta the cabbage patch, Pug!"

With the gun in his spine, Ed entered the small office.

The two men whom Ed had seen from outside were thugs

he knew by name. One was Hymie Sykes, the other was Barney Tortola. They were busy spreading cotton waste on the floor. Tortola was spreading the cotton, and Sykes was pouring gasoline on it.

In the corner, Pug Lester sat on a chair, very handsome and cool, supervising the operation. Alongside him lay two figures, both securely bound with wire and gagged. One was a young man of about nineteen or twenty. The other was Elspeth Sinclair.

"Nice work, Leo," Pug Lester said to the man who had Ed Race covered. "I figured he'd manage to get here somehow." He got up from his chair lazily, caressing the butt of a small automatic pistol. He was still in evening clothes. "You certainly kept putting wrenches in the works for me all night, Race."

Ed grinned at him, still feeling Leo's gun in his spine. "I just put another wrench in your works, Pug. I 'phoned the cops to send a radio car over here. They'll arrive any minute."

Lester smiled and shook his head. "Wrong, Race. Didn't you hear the fire-engines just now? That was one of my joints burning. My boys started that fire, and it'll be occupying the cops in the radio car. They'll be over there, holding back the crowd, and not even in their car, so they won't hear the radio. They won't get the order to come here—and they won't come. How do you like that?"

"I don't like it," Ed said. "What are you going to do—cremate Elspeth and her brother, alive?"

"You got the idea, Race. And as long as you're here, you can join them. It'll be a hot time in the old town tonight." He motioned to Tortola and Sykes. "Get his guns while Leo keeps him covered. And see if he's got that forty grand too."

"Wait a minute," said Ed. "You're a sap for staging this, Pug. It's too complicated. Something is bound to slip."

Pug Lester grinned. "How do you know it's complicated?"

"I can guess," Ed told him. "That skunk, Courtney Sinclair—Elspeth's cousin—must owe you plenty of jack. Maybe he lost it at your tables, and gave you notes."

"So what?" Lester asked softly. His eyes were glittering. "So what?"

"So this," Ed went on. "The only way Courtney Sinclair can get enough dough to pay you off, is if he inherits it from his old crab of an uncle, Warren Sinclair. But he can't inherit, because Sinclair has two children of his own—Elspeth here, and her brother, Austin. So you decide to fix it for Courtney to inherit. You kidnap Austin, and demand forty grand ransom. Elspeth is ordered to deliver the dough to a blind beggar on Forty-Eighth Street. She's afraid to tell her father, because old Warren is so tight he won't pay forty grand to get his son back. He'll notify the police, and Elspeth is afraid her brother will get knocked off by the kidnapers. So what happens, but her big, handsome friend—that's you, Pug—comes along and offers to lend her the forty grand to pay the ransom. You just do that to make everything look kosher.

"**SHE PAYS** off, and is supposed to get word where to find her brother. Some mug contacts her in your club and gives her this address. You let her go alone, so you can prove you weren't the one to see her alive last. She comes here, you follow her—

the crowd at your night club probably thinks you're still in your office—and now you're setting a little fire. All they'll find will be charred bodies of Austin and Elspeth... and cousin Courtney inherits and pays you off!"

While Ed talked, he had been standing tautly, every muscle tight and steel-springed. He had no leeway against that gun of Leo's in his spine.

Any move he made would release a bullet from Leo's gun, and he'd be through—and Pug Lester's little game would go ahead as scheduled.

Pug Lester's face was white and cold. "Every word you say is true, Race. You've called every turn. Now see if you can call the next turn. Take him, boys!"

Tortola and Sykes moved over toward him, Sykes picking up a length of picture-wire. To reach him they had to step over the gasoline-soaked cotton waste on the floor, and to pass within a few feet of Elspeth Sinclair.

She was bound and helpless, but Ed saw grim determination in her violet eyes. That girl wasn't licked yet. She made a convulsive movement with her body that sent her rolling over against Tortola's legs. Her rolling body struck him from behind, and he staggered, into Sykes.

"Hey!" yelled Sykes.

For an instant, Ed felt Leo's gun relax against his spine. That was all the break he wanted. His body twisted in a swift spiral, with elbows hard against his side. His right elbow made a battering-ram which smashed against Leo at the same time that it took Ed's spine out of line with the gun.

Then Ed came all the way around, bringing his left fist, bunched and hard, in a smashing blow.

Leo dropped the gun and went staggering backward.

Ed kept moving. He went forward into a head-on somersault, just as three guns barked in unison. Pug Lester, Hymie Sykes and Barney Tortola were all shooting. But Ed was coming out of his somersault six feet away, over in the far corner, with two blasting .45's in his hands.

He shot to kill, and without mercy. He emptied ten shots out of those two guns, and each slug found its mark in the body of one of those men. He could have stopped after the third shot, but he was filled with a terrible and consuming hatred of these cold-blooded murderers.

At last his guns were empty, and no men stood before him.

He stepped among the bloody, battered bodies on the floor, and came to the side of Elspeth Sinclair. He stooped, pulled the gag from her mouth, unbound the picture-wire. Then he did the same for young Austin Sinclair.

Austin was a wiry kid, and he didn't seem to be much the worse for wear.

But Elspeth was shivering, as with the ague. Ed Race put an arm around her to support her. She was suddenly overcome by a great weakness, and her head buried itself on his shoulder.

She raised her eyes to his. "Forgive me for treating you so shabbily at my house," she whispered. "I—I thought—"

"Never mind what you thought," he said. "You did a swell job when you rolled into Tortola. It was the break we needed.

I'm thinking, young lady, that you and I could work very well together."

"I'm sure we could!"

Ed Race's muscles were always coördinated to react to any emergency. They did not fail him this time. He bent his head and kissed her.

DEATH'S BOOKING AGENT

TIMES SQUARE hadn't changed much in the two years that Ed Race had been away on his coast-to-coast vaudeville tour. There were the same flaring electric signs, the same crowds, the same bustling and shoving. A few new restaurants, yes. And some familiar faces missing. But the Main Stem was largely the same.

Ed breathed in large gulps of Broadway air, and liked it. He was standing in front of "Frenchy's" Cigar Store and looking directly across the maze of traffic at the marquee of the Clyde Theatre, where they were changing the letters on the electric sign to announce next week's show. They were putting *him* up there. He was the star attraction at the Clyde for next week. It was many years since Ed had first seen his name go up in electric lights, but he always got a renewed thrill out of it. The sign read:

THE MASKED MARKSMAN
The Man Who Can Make Guns Talk!

The general public didn't know the true identity of the Masked Marksman, but the insiders on Broadway knew, and Ed received many a happy greeting as old friends passed.

Abruptly, he became tense. He was conscious that a hand had been surreptitiously inserted in his right coat pocket.

His first instinct was to whirl around and catch the thief's

Ed Race acted instinctively. He thrust out his foot and spilled the first detective. The second one sprawled over his partner....

hand. But he held himself in check, a curious smile tugging at his lips. He had, perhaps, eighty or ninety cents in the change pocket there. Let the fellow get it. He was obviously an amateur. To create a scene would bring the police, and the poor chap would get ninety days in the workhouse. Ed was the last one in the world to encourage crime—but he didn't want to be responsible for sending a pickpocket to jail. There were plenty of more vicious criminals who needed attention.

The hand was still in his pocket, apparently having trouble. This was certainly no experienced pickpocket. An expert would have been in and out long ago, with the swag.

At last the hand was withdrawn.

Ed decided he'd like to get a look at the bloke who had taken his eighty cents. His eyes widened as he turned around.

It was a girl.

She had fluffy blonde hair. She was wearing a light summer dress. Her face was small, the features clear and perfect like those of a Dresden doll. Her eyes were sea-blue, and there was terror in them.

She met Ed Race's glance, and uttered a frightened gasp as she darted away into the moving throng of pedestrians. Ed got a quick glimpse of her hands. They were long and slender—and empty. Not even a purse.

She hadn't taken anything, after all!

Ed touched his pocket and frowned. Instead of taking anything—*she had put something in!*

His fingers touched paper-currency. It was a package of hundred dollar bills—flecked with blood!

He felt the sudden exhilaration which always came to him when life presented him with mystery or excitement. He had been following the girl with his eyes as she darted through the crowd, heading for the doorway of the Scrogg Building. He started to follow her, and then stopped short as he heard a familiar, unpleasant voice behind him.

"There she is, Monk! Grab her, quick!"

HE KNEW without looking, that the voice belonged to Detective Sergeant Lomas and the instructions were directed at First Grade Detective Monk. Those two were the most despicable team of cops on the Broadway beat. Among police, as among every other class, there were good and bad. It had been

Ed's experience that in New York's police force the good far outweighed the bad. But a pair like Lomas and Monk went far to mar the reputation of an otherwise clean and honest body of men.

Ed wasn't sure how they had got their assignment to the Broadway squad. There had been wire-pulling somewhere, and it was suspected that they owed their jobs to the influence of Luke Bilbo. It was Bilbo who had taken over the vice and narcotic empire of Lucky Luciano. He modernized and streamlined it so that it ran just as efficiently as ever before, if not quite so blatantly.

Ed wouldn't have relished the thought of a stray dog at the mercy of those two strong-arm dicks—much less the thought of that blonde, fragile girl with the frightened eyes.

He heard Monk's wheezing breath as he brushed past, and the urgent voice of Sergeant Lomas yelling behind him: *"Hold that girl! Stop, you, or we'll shoot!"*

He saw the girl hesitate in the doorway of the Scrogg Building, not knowing which way to flee, for there was no back entrance. Once inside, she'd be cornered.

Ed Race acted upon instinct alone. He thrust out a left foot, and tripped Detective Pete Monk, who went sprawling into a crowd of people. Lomas, who was close on his heels, fell over him, and the two of them scrambled awkwardly on the ground. For some reason, they had drawn their guns, though God knows there was little enough necessity for weapons in apprehending a frail and frightened girl.

Monk's gun went flying out of his hand, but Lomas held on

to his. He squirmed up to his feet, and a look like the bowels of hell disfigured his ugly face.

Ed looked over in the girl's direction, and nodded to her, reassuringly. She flashed him a grateful, half-frightened glance, and darted into a cab which was parked at the curb. The door slammed and the taxi pulled away, while Ed wondered a second what she was going to use for money to pay the fare. He was sure that the girl was as innocent and guileless as a newborn babe. The fact that Lomas and Monk wanted her proved she couldn't be guilty of anything terrible—even though she had shoved a package of bloody money into his pocket.

And he was sure of another thing. That she hadn't chosen him by accident to be the recipient of that money. There must be five thousand dollars in that package. She wouldn't have stuck it in any stranger's pocket, no matter how desperate she was. Ed reasoned that she must be a member of the theatrical fraternity, and probably knew him by sight. Among the troopers on Broadway there were hundreds whom Ed Race had never met, but to whom he was known. And the one thing they could always be sure of was that he would never refuse to help a fellow Thespian in trouble.

But now—right at this minute, *he* was in a jam.

SERGEANT LOMAS was on his feet holding the service revolver in a tight grip. Behind him, Monk was getting to his feet, and looking around for his gun.

Lomas's face was black with anger. He waggled the revolver at Ed. "You tripped us on purpose, damn you, Race!" he bellowed. "You deliberately made us lose that dame!"

Ed Race looked hurt. "*Sergeant* Lomas! How can you say such a thing? You and Monk should look where you're running."

"Yeah? You lie, you dirty son—"

He stopped abruptly, seeing the look in Ed Race's cold gray eyes.

Perhaps he remembered that Race had plenty of connections in New York, too. And possibly he remembered that Ed Race carried two heavy forty-five caliber revolvers in his shoulder holsters, and could use them as no man had ever before been able to use them. Lomas knew who Ed was. He knew that every night, six nights a week for the last ten years Ed Race juggled six of those forty-five caliber, hair-trigger revolvers in his act in the various top-notch vaudeville theatres all over the country. And catching those dangerous weapons as they came down into his hands, he fired each one successively at a row of candles thirty feet across the stage. In ten years the Masked Marksman had never missed one of them. A noted millionaire had once followed him from theatre to theatre, betting that he would miss once before the tour was over. The millionaire had lost.

Lomas had also seen the second number of Ed's show, where he came on to the stage empty-handed, with a girl assistant who had a handful of silver dollars. The girl would begin to flip them into the air in front of a padded mattress. Ed would go into a back somersault. When he came out of it, he had two revolvers in his hands, miraculously drawn from their holsters while he was somersaulting. And those revolvers would start barking before he landed on his feet. With each thunderous explosion, another of the spinning silver dollars would be smashed into the mattress.

Perhaps it was that amazing draw of Ed's which Lomas remembered, and which kept his ugly temper in check. He swallowed hard.

"That dame is wanted for murder, wise guy. She just stabbed Douglas Mayberry to death, in his office, and grabbed five grand. If it hadn't been for you, we'd of nabbed her!"

A crowd was gathering around them, listening eagerly.

Ed made a clucking sound. "*Tsk, tsk.* How do you know she killed Mayberry?"

Lomas glared at him. "How do we know? Because she had the dough with her, that's how. There's blood on that money—Mayberry's."

"How do you know she had the money?" Ed persisted.

Lomas's face became apoplectically red. "How do we know? By God, Race, I think you're in cahoots with her! I'll show you—"

In his bursting anger, he forgot for a moment what he knew about Race's reputation. He raised his revolver to slash with the sights at Ed's face. "You punk, I'll show you—"

And then something strange and mystifying happened. To the bystanders who were watching avidly, it seemed that the tall man with the cold gray eyes had not moved at all. Yet, miraculously, a heavy, forty-five caliber revolver appeared in his hand. It must have come out of his shoulder holster, but no one had seen it come. Like a blur before their eyes, that forty-five flashed upward to meet the down-slash of Lomas's gun-hand.

The sergeant's wrist struck against the barrel of Ed's gun, and his hand went limp. A look of pain crossed his thick face, and the service revolver fell from nerveless fingers.

Lomas's face was a twisted mask of hatred. He glanced sideways and gasped hoarsely, "*You* take him, Monk!"

Unseen by Ed, Detective Pete Monk-had recovered his gun. He felt it in his right side and heard Monk grate: "Resisting an officer, huh!"

ED RACE knew by the vicious glint in Monk's eyes that he was going to pull the trigger. These two hated him, and here was the best chance they'd ever have. The street was full of bystanders who would testify that Ed Race had drawn a gun. What more justification would they need for shooting him down?

Now Ed Race did a thing which he did every night on the vaudeville stage before a paying audience. Only here, the audience was free, and his life was at stake.

He went into a back somersault.

He moved with dazzling speed, into the back flip. His left hand touched the ground, and his feet came up to complete the somersault, just as Monk's gun exploded. That swift and puzzling action had spoiled the dick's aim. The bullet went a foot wide of the mark, and chipped plaster off the entrance of the Scrogg Building.

Monk's lips were twisted in a snarl as he swung his muzzle after Ed's body for a second shot.

But he never got in that second shot, because Ed Race was already coming out of the somersault, and his heavy forty-five spat flame in a belching explosion as he fired a snapshot. The bullet smashed into the stock of Monk's service revolver. It went hurtling out of his grip, while the detective stood with a stupid expression on his face, staring down at his numbed and empty hand.

A babel of shouts arose from the crowd around them. "My Gawd!" yelled a man. "That must be the Masked Marksman! Ain't no one but the Masked Marksman can shoot like that!"

Ed holstered his gun, and faced the two detectives. "Well, gentlemen," he asked courteously, "was there anything else you wanted?"

Sergeant Lomas was holding his sprained wrist, and the looks he was darting at Ed might have been barbed with poison.

"You're damn right there is! You're under arrest—"

He stopped, swallowing hard, as a level cold, authoritative voice interrupted him. "What's going on here?"

Ed Race's face lighted up. "Mac!" he exclaimed. He turned to meet the calm but friendly gaze of Inspector MacSpain.

MacSpain was a powerfully built man, with iron-gray hair and a pair of shrewd eyes which saw everything and were fooled by nothing. He and Ed had been friends for years, ever since the old days when Patrolman MacSpain had walked a beat on the East Side, and let a kid named Eddie Race touch his service revolver with loving and reverent fingers. They had both come far since those days. And it was partly because of MacSpain that Ed Race had turned to the study of criminology as a hobby.

Ed's contract with the Partages Circuit paid him enough money so that he could have lived on the fat of the land. Instead, his nervous energy and his craving for excitement had driven him to take up the pursuit of criminology as a sideline. He held licenses to act as a private detective in a dozen states, and there had been more than one occasion when he had helped his friend to obtain promotion with the aid of his famous forty-fives.

"Hello, Eddie," MacSpain said sourly. "You in trouble again?"

Ed Race didn't have a chance to answer because Sergeant Lomas burst in. "I've just placed him under arrest, Inspector. He attacked me, and fired at Monk, here!"

MacSpain raised his eyebrows. "You don't say! How come?"

"We were chasing a dame for the murder of Douglas Mayberry. He helped her to escape. Besides the charge of resisting an officer, I charge him with aiding and abetting a fugitive!"

There was a gleam of triumph in Lomas' eyes. He knew of the friendship between these two men, and he hated MacSpain as much as he hated Ed Race. He was glad of the chance to rub it in, and added spitefully, "I suspect that he's implicated in Mayberry's murder!"

Inspector MacSpain raised his eyebrows. He looked at Ed. "Are you?"

Ed grinned. "Not guilty."

Lomas shook a finger in his face. "Then why did you try to help that girl to escape?"

"Why did you and your pal trip over my foot?"

Lomas spread his hands in a gesture of resignation. "You see, Inspector, he admits that he tripped us. I insist on taking him in on suspicion of complicity in May-berry's murder. Maybe if we search him, we'll find incriminating evidence on him."

ED FELT a chill in his bones. If they found that blood-stained money on him, Lomas would crucify him.

MacSpain was plainly in a dilemma. As Inspector of Homicide, it was his duty to hold Ed. With the charge which Lomas had placed against him, he would have held any other suspect. But he was sure that his old friend had not murdered Mayberry.

Ed solved the problem for him. "I'd like to oblige you, Lomas, but I can't take the time to be arrested right now. I've got a midnight show at the Clyde in an hour and a half. But I'll tell you what—I'll come down to headquarters after the show, and you can give me the third degree if you want."

MacSpain smiled. "I'm sure we can do that." He glared at Lomas. "Ed Race is well-known in New York. He certainly isn't going to run away on us."

"All right," Lomas said reluctantly. "But only on one condition—that Detective Monk stays with him every minute of the time. I want to make sure he doesn't meet that girl!"

"Okay!" Ed agreed. He clapped MacSpain on the shoulder. "Better be down at headquarters later, Mac. I hate to trust myself with that baby in the third degree room. I might beat him up!"

Lomas scowled, and MacSpain grinned, as Ed started across the street, with Pete Monk at his elbow.

"Remember, Monk," Lomas bawled after them, "that Race is in custody!"

"I'll remember, all right!" Monk growled, giving Ed a dirty look.

Ed refrained from mentioning to MacSpain, Monk's practically deliberate attempt to kill him. He was aware of the amount of drag possessed by Lomas and Monk, and he didn't want to cause his friend any unnecessary embarrassment. Ed felt able to fend off any other attempt which Monk might make.

They started to cross the street, and he noticed a showy sedan drawn up at the curb, with the short-wave radio going full blast.

Ed knew both the men sitting in that car. The flashily dressed, hawk-faced man on the near side was Luke Bilbo, the vice czar whose vicious organization had secured Lomas and Monk their jobs. The one behind the wheel—with the twitching nether lip and the shifty eyes—was known in the underworld as Dopey Leo.

Although it had never been proved, Dopey Leo was said to be Luke Bilbo's knife-man. Bilbo didn't use trigger men in the manner of Lucky Luciano, Dutch Schultz, and the old order of mobsters. Guns made too much noise, attracted too much attention, and were too easy to check by ballistics. Knife men were effective. A knife is silent, and you don't need a permit to carry one, and it can't be traced. In six months, fourteen men had died from stab wounds. The rumor was, that Dopey Leo had collected five grand a piece for those killings. And, by a strange coincidence, several of the murdered men had been competitors of Bilbo—aspirants to his vice throne.

BILBO LEANED out. His dark, hawk-face was inscrutable. "Hello, Race," he said.

Monk slowed down as Ed paused alongside the car. Dopey Leo was fiddling with the radio. He turned it up high, moving it from the short-wave to the regular band and catching a news announcer:

"... Douglas Mayberry, the Broadway loan broker, was stabbed to death at 10:25 this evening. The murderer escaped, leaving the knife in his victim's body. Police are investigating, and we hope to have another flash for you in a short while. Keep tuned to this station...."

Bilbo scowled. "Turn it off, Dopey!"

"Okay, doke, Boss!" chirped Leo, with a smirk. He twirled the knob, choking off the announcer.

Bilbo looked up at Ed Race, and winked broadly to Monk. "This the guy that killed Mayberry, Pete?"

"I dunno, Luke," Monk growled. "Maybe we'll pin it on him yet, at that."

"Wasn't there a dame?" Bilbo asked Monk.

"Yeah. But she got away. It was that Selma Williams girl. She or her brother did it. And Race, here, helped her escape."

Ed Race went taut at mention of the girl's name. Now he knew who she was. Evan Williams was one of the greatest acrobats the vaudeville stage had ever seen. Ed had shared billings with him on many occasions. And Evan had always talked about his kid sister, Selma, whom Ed had never met. But she would certainly know him, from the picture which Evan had at home. That's how she had recognized him. But what in the world would Evan Williams, or his sister, have to do with the loan shark, Douglas Mayberry? Williams had plenty of money—

His thoughts were interrupted by the drawling voice of Luke Bilbo. "Well, Race, I hope you squirm out of this one—on a marble slab!"

Dopey Leo, sitting next to his boss, began to laugh. "Haw,

haw! That's rich! On a marble slab! That's in the morgue! Boss, you tickle me!"

Bilbo grinned thinly. "Shut up, Leo," he said over his shoulder.

Ed looked down speculatively at Bilbo. "Where were you and Leo at ten-twenty-five?" he asked softly.

Luke Bilbo stopped laughing abruptly. "Another crack like that out of you, Race, and—"

"Yes?" Ed asked, his eyes suddenly icy cold. "Yes, Bilbo?"

The vice czar lowered his eyes quickly. "It's up to the cops to question me," he grumbled. "Not you. If you know where that girl is, you better tell Monk."

"Why?" Ed asked. "Why do you want to know? So you can have Dopey knock her off?"

Bilbo's face flushed, but he didn't answer. Dopey Leo was looking at Ed with glittering eyes. His hand was hidden under his coat. "Mister Race," he said, "someday I'm gonna carve your liver right outta you!"

"You're welcome to try, Leo," Ed told him. "But don't forget to bring your own coffin along."

Bilbo was watching Ed with narrowed eyes. "I've often wondered about that," he whispered. "You know, I really think Leo could throw his knife faster than you could shoot, Race!"

Ed grinned. "Bring him up on the Clyde stage some night. We'll have a match!"

He turned and strode away, with the sour-looking Monk at his elbow.

Instead of crossing directly to the Clyde, however, he angled diagonally up toward Forty-ninth Street.

"Hey!" protested Monk. "You're at the Clyde Theatre. Where you going?"

"To my hotel, to change, and pick up my other guns."

Monk accepted the explanation, and accompanied him over to the Longmont, where Ed invariably stayed when in New York. They always gave him the same room, 716, and his key was always available at the desk to anyone whom the clerk knew to be a friend of Ed's. Anyone with a worry on his mind, a problem to solve, or a touch to make, was sure of a welcome when Ed was in town.

Monk glowered as they went up in the elevator, but he said nothing. On the seventh floor he marched side by side with him to the door of 716, and watched morosely while Ed unlocked the door.

ED PUSHED in first, blocking the doorway with his broad shoulders. He took one look into the room, and smiled wryly. He had been afraid of this. Selma Williams was sitting on his bed.

There was a smile on her face and she started to say something, but smothered her words at sight of the frown on Ed's face. He stopped short in the doorway and Pete Monk came up against him.

"What the hell is the idea—" Monk glowered.

"Mr. Monk," Ed said apologetically, "I assure you I am very sorry to have to do this."

"Do what?"

"This!"

Ed brought his right fist up from the hip, and it landed flush on Monk's jaw. The detective's head jerked back and his eyes went glassy.

"Shut the door, quick!" he ordered Selma.

"O-oh!" she breathed. "That—that's the detective that was chasing me! You hit him!"

"Yes," said Ed. "I hit him." He plopped Monk onto the bed, and went to rummage in the closet. He returned in a moment with a spare garter. He wadded a handkerchief over Monk's mouth, and then tied it with the garter, making a very effective gag. Then he twisted Monk's hands behind his back, and manacled him to the bedstead with his own police handcuffs.

He turned away from Monk and faced the girl. For a long minute he looked down into her sea-blue eyes.

"Tell me, child. Did you stab Douglas Mayberry to death?"

Her eyes widened like saucers. She shuddered. "No! No!"

"Who killed him?"

"God help me, I don't know!"

"Why did you put the package of money in my pocket?"

He took it out and held it up before her.

She made no attempt to touch it. The blood stains seemed to fascinate her so that she was speechless for a minute. At last she gulped, and stammered, "I—I f-found it—beside Mayberry's body. There were f-fingerprints—bloody fingerprints on the bills, and I thought they might be the killer's p-prints, so I t-took it."

"You poor little kid," he said. "Didn't you know the prints would be rubbed off?"

"I—I didn't think of it. I—I was afraid. Those detectives were chasing me, and I w-was frightened. I saw you, and it s-seemed to be a good idea to p-put it in your pocket and come and get it later."

"Selma," he asked quietly, "are you sure you don't know who killed Mayberry?"

"Y-yes."

"Did your brother—Evan—kill him? Weren't you trying to get rid of the package because you thought it might have Evan's fingerprints?"

He felt her slender body stiffen, as her two little hands rose to her breasts. She stared up at him, wide-eyed, and a tortured sob gushed from her throat.

Ed let her chin drop, and turned away. He took a bottle of Canadian whiskey from the dresser. He poured some in a glass and added a little water.

"Drink that," he told her.

She gulped the liquor, and coughed, but the color came back to her cheeks.

"All right, Selma," Ed said quietly. "Now tell me all about it."

She looked at him piteously. "If—if Evan killed Douglas Mayberry—w-would you help him—to escape?"

"Not to escape, my child," Ed told her gently. "I know Evan too well. There'd be no peace for him anywhere as a hunted man. But I give you my word I'll get him the best lawyer in the country. He'll have every chance. There must have been some reason—"

"No, no, you mustn't say that. I—I'm not sure Evan killed him. Evan came home drunk tonight—"

"Drunk?" Ed's voice held an edge of surprise. Williams never drank.

"Yes. Evan was drunk, and fighting mad. He'd been out of town, and while he was away, I got a job—with Mayberry. Evan hated and despised Mayberry, and had warned him once, to keep away from me. But I thought I should support myself, so when Mayberry offered me the job in his loan office, I took it. Evan found out when he got back from a tour this morning, and he w-went to see Mayberry. He came home drunk, and said something about having had a fight. Then he passed out. I—I was scared, so I dressed and went over there. And—"

SHE SOBBED, and covered her face with her hands.

Ed patted her shoulder. "You found Douglas Mayberry stabbed to death, eh? And you naturally assumed that Evan had killed him?"

She nodded dumbly.

"The knife was in his back?"

"Y-yes."

"What happened then?"

"I—I saw the money, and picked it up, and hurried out. Just as I got to the street, those two detectives—Monk, here and that other one, came toward the building. They saw me with the money, and the other one whispered to Monk. Then they chased me. I was scared they'd find the money with Evan's fingerprints on it, so I ran."

"I see," Ed said thoughtfully. Suddenly he straightened. "All right, Selma. I'm going to see your brother. Where is he?"

She gave him the address of the boarding house on Fifty-third Street where they lived. "What—what are you going to do?"

"I'll have to talk to him before I decide. In the meantime, you stay here—"

"No. I want to go with you—"

"Impossible, Selma. There'll be an alarm out for you."

He thrust the package of money in his pocket and took a black chamois case from his dresser drawer. It contained four more revolvers. They were the guns he used in his Masked Marksman act. He picked out one of them and gave it to Selma.

"You sit right here in this chair, and keep this gun. If Monk gets loose, or if anyone tries to break in, *shoot!*"

She nodded, holding the gun gingerly.

"It's a hair trigger," he told her. "Be careful of it."

He left her sitting in the chair, and went to open the door.

He stepped back, with an oath as three men barged in. Sergeant Lomas was in the lead. Luke Bilbo and Dopey Leo were behind him.

Sergeant Lomas and Luke Bilbo had guns in their hands, and Dopey Leo held a long, glittering knife.

Bilbo kicked the door shut behind them as Lomas stuck a gun against Ed's chest.

"Put your hands up, Race!" he grated. "You're under arrest! Make a single move, and I'll blast you!"

ED BACKED up, with his hands in the air. Lomas wasn't fooling. There was no doubt that he'd shoot if Ed made a move.

He dipped his hand into Ed's pocket, and brought out the blood-stained package of money. "Here we are, boys!"

Dopey Leo licked his lips, and fastened his glittering eyes on Ed. "Boss," he asked, "how much will you pay me to carve this mugg up for you?"

"Shut up!" Bilbo grated. "You've done enough damage for one day!"

Ed kept his hands raised shoulder high, and looked square in Lomas' eyes. "It wasn't the girl you wanted, was it, Lomas? It was just that package of money!"

Lomas didn't answer. His eyes were mere pinpoints. But Bilbo spoke. "Smart, aren't you, Race? You know what we wanted the dough for?"

"Sure I do. You paid Dopey Leo, here, to kill Douglas Mayberry. He got himself coked up and went and stabbed him to death. But while he was doing it, he dropped this package of money—the five grand you had paid him for the murder."

Watching Bilbo, he knew he had hit the truth.

He went on. "Dopey told you about it, but he was afraid to go back and get the money. You were afraid Dopey's prints would be on the bills. So you got hold of Lomas and Monk in a hurry and sent them to retrieve the package."

Bilbo's eyes flickered. He glanced at Lomas. "Too bad, isn't it?"

Ed nodded. "I thought you'd see it that way. Are you going to kill us both?"

"Yeah. For resisting arrest."

ED'S EYES had flicked over to Selma. He realized that she had reached under the cushion and was gripping the heavy revolver he had given her. There wasn't a chance that she could shoot it out with both Lomas and Bilbo, and escape Leo's knife.

But he could tell from the glint in her eyes that she was going to try.

"*Throw it to me!*" Ed shouted, and went into a back somersault.

Lomas's gun exploded, but Ed was no longer there!

Ed had no gun, but he hoped desperately that Selma had understood his order. As he came to his feet his eyes flicked toward her, and he saw the revolver spinning through the air in his direction.

She had understood!

Bilbo's gun cracked, and Lomas' revolver spat flame, almost simultaneously. But Ed had dived head-first toward the spinning gun, and their shots smashed into the wall where he had been but a second before. Now he caught the revolver in midair, and went into a forward somersault.

He pulled the trigger only three times, but each shot did its duty. Lomas was smashed back against the wall with a slug in his forehead, and Bilbo took one high in the chest.

Dopey Leo's arm was moving forward in a dexterous knife-cast, when Ed's shot struck him in the right shoulder. He dropped the knife and yelled, "Don't shoot no more! I'll talk!"

Ed was breathing regularly, showing no exertion from his double somersault. Monk, still handcuffed, lay on the bed, wide-eyed. Selma Williams had not moved from the chair. Her eyes were shining as she looked at Ed. "I—I never—saw such shooting!"

Ed grinned down at her. "Come to the Clyde tonight and you'll see more of it!"

There was a pounding at the door. Ed crossed and opened it, to admit MacSpain.

The Inspector looked around the room as he pulled at his ear. "My God, Eddie," he said, "are you still in trouble? I saw these bozos go up in the elevator. It looks like I'm a little late."

"Not at all, Mac," Ed said. "You're just in time to take over. Dopey Leo here, wants to talk. And I've got to go."

He went over to the dresser and once more took out the chamois case, then he picked up his two revolvers which Lomas had taken from him. He took Selma by the arm, led her to the door.

"Where the hell do you think you're going?" MacSpain demanded.

Ed grinned. "Did you forget I have a midnight show at the Clyde?"

"Well, I'll be damned!" said MacSpain.

"Me, too!" Dopey Leo said gloomily.

BANK-NIGHT FOR CORPSES

ED RACE lit a cigar, and took three long puffs at it, to get the tip glowing. Then he flipped it high up into the air. It sailed straight upward like a comet, with sparks flashing from it. He turned in leisurely fashion, bowed to the audience, and spread his empty hands in a gesture requesting quiet.

Abe Selden, down in the pit, held his baton rigid, and the orchestra's low melody died away into silence. Not a sound was to be heard in the packed theatre, as the glowing cigar reached the height of its parabola, high up over the stage, and began to fall, with the burning tip aimed downward. Now it resembled an aerial torpedo-bomb descending upon a selected target. The audience was tense.

Ed Race smiled genially. He adjusted the small mask which covered the upper part of his face. He seemed to be in no hurry whatsoever.

And then, when the falling cigar was barely fifteen feet from the floor of the stage, he suddenly went into a flurry of motion. He turned sideways to the audience, facing the other end of the stage, where that glowing tip was visible in the spotlight which had been suddenly focused upon it. He threw his lithe body backward, into a back somersault. The tips of his fingers touched the floor of the stage as he went heels-over-head, then

Those shots were the last the gunmen ever fired…

landed upon his feet. Miraculously—uncannily—a heavy .45 caliber revolver appeared in one hand.

As his feet touched the floor and his body straightened, that revolver roared once thunderously, belching flame.

The gaping audience saw the falling cigar jerk under the impact of the heavy slug, which smashed it back into the thick asbestos mattress at the other end of the stage. The orchestra sounded a single chord as accompaniment to the shot, and then became immediately silent again.

Ed Race holstered the revolver with a lightning-like motion, and strode across the stage. In front of the mattress, he stooped and picked up the cigar. He held it aloft for all to see.

The tip of that cigar was all torn and shredded. Where the glowing end had been, but a moment before, there was now only a pulpy mass of shredded tobacco. The Masked Marksman had shot away the burning tip of a falling cigar—in the air!

A slow ripple of applause arose from the balcony, and spread throughout the house, gaining volume until it reached a thunderous crescendo of tempestuous approval.

This was the climax of the Masked Marksman's vaudeville act. From coast to coast, on the far-flung stages of the Partages Circuit, it had never failed to bring down the house. And now, here on the stage of the great Clyde Theatre on Broadway, the wonder of his marvelous shooting skill carried away even the blasé New York audience.

Truly, the Masked Marksman was living up to the legend which appeared under his name on the marquee outside—*The Man Who Can Make Guns Talk!*

In his twelve years on the vaudeville stage Ed Race had bowed thus, before thousands of wildly applauding audiences. Yet each time he got a renewed thrill out of it. The same warm, glowing feeling always arose in his heart as he bowed once to the swelling tumult of applause, and began to back out into the wing.

And then, he stiffened with surprise. Behind the small black mask, his gray eyes narrowed; a twinkle appeared in them at sight of the chubby little boy who had come running out on the stage from the opposite wing. The little tyke was no more than six years old, and his head was covered with a profusion of golden curls. His round little face was smeared with dirt, and full of tense excitement.

BEHIND THE lad, the assistant stage manager was running, trying to catch him, and yelling, "Come here, sonny! My Gawd, you can't go out there—"

But the lad was already out on the stage, and the stage manager dared not follow him. The audience stopped applauding, and started to laugh good-naturedly.

The golden-haired little lad didn't even notice the packed house. He ran straight across the stage, with his arms stretched out to Ed Race.

Ed smiled. He stooped and picked the boy up.

"Chubby Warren!" he whispered. "How the devil did you get in here, Chubby?"

"I ducked past the doorkeeper, Eddie," the boy gasped, breathless. "Aunt Mary sent me. She—she said to bring you right over. We—we're in trouble!"

Ed grinned. He patted Chubby Warren on the head, and turned to face the audience. Out of the corner of his eye he saw the stage manager and many of the actors and stage-hands crowding in the wings, wondering how he—would handle the situation. Tom Nolan, the assistant stage manager, had his hand on the lever, ready to ring down the curtain, but Ed shook his head slightly. He smiled, and bowed to the house, with Chubby still in his arms.

"Ladies and gentlemen," he said, "meet my mascot. He hopes to be a gunman when he grows up!"

Laughter rippled through the house, and Ed backed off the stage. Now he nodded to Tom Nolan, and the curtain came down.

While the next number went on, everybody backstage crowded around Ed and Chubby. Tom Nolan came over, frowning, but Ed said, "Leave the kid alone, Tom. Don't you know him? He's Chubby Warren—Ted Warren's kid!"

Everybody knew the name of Ted Warren. He had been a trapeze performer on the Partages Circuit, and had been killed in a thirty-foot dive while doing a daring acrobatic act, right here in the Clyde Theatre. That was four years ago. He had left a pair of gorgeous twins, two years old—Chubby and Nora. Their mother had died a year before. Ted Warren's younger sister, Mary, had taken over the raising of the twins. With a sum of money contributed by generous old Leon Partages, Mary Warren had opened a small photographic supply store on Forty-sixth Street, and the theatrical fraternity went out of their way to patronize her. They sent her films to develop and print, from wherever they were on tour, and she would follow their schedules and mail the prints so as to reach them at their next stop.

Chubby Warren wriggled in Ed's arms and looked a little bewildered and scared by all the people who were crowding around them. He put his month close to Ed's ear and whispered, "Please, Uncle Ed, let's get out of here, quick. Aunt Mary says if you don't come right away something terrible may happen to Sis."

Ed stiffened. He saw now, that Chubby was wearing his pajamas under his little coat, and that the lad's feet were clad only in bedroom slippers. It was after ten at night, and Chubby should be in bed. That Mary Warren had routed him out and sent him to the Clyde to get Ed Race, meant that there was real trouble.

"Okay, Chubby," he said. "We're on our way!"

He pushed through the actors and stage hands crowding around them, and made for the stage door. He pulled the mask from his face, and stuffed it in his pocket. Otherwise, he was ready for the street. He always appeared on the stage in street clothes, without make-up. The only thing he used was the mask, and six forty-five caliber revolvers, two of which he always carried in shoulder holsters under his arms.

AS HE hurried toward the exit, still carrying Chubby, he asked, "What's the trouble, kid? Why did Aunt Mary send you for me?"

"Gosh, Uncle Ed, I don't know. Some bad men came to the house, and took Sis away with them. Two of them stayed in the house, and I heard them talking to Aunt Mary in the next room, and then she came into the bedroom and whispered to me to get some clothes on and sneak into the kitchen and down the dumbwaiter, and go and get you. So I did that, and here I am."

Ed felt his blood racing. Little Nora Warren, Chubby's twin sister—taken away by "bad men"! Chubby sneaking down the dumbwaiter to come looking for Ed Race!

"Come on, Chubby!" Ed exclaimed, pushing out into the street. "We'll get the police—"

"Oh, no, Uncle Ed! Aunt Mary said especially to tell you—not to call the police!"

Ed's mouth formed a tight, thin line. He turned left on Forty-sixth, without putting Chubby down. The stage entrance of the Clyde was on Forty-sixth Street, only half a block down from the Warren Photographic Shop. The street was quiet. It was that in-between time in the theatrical district, when the streets are empty, and the theatres filled. There were only one or two pedestrians, and a couple of cabs cruising lazily, and Ed could see a car parked half way down the block in front of the Warren Photographic Shop.

Just at that moment, two men came running out of that building. They stopped for a moment under the modest neon sign which read:

DEVELOPING & PRINTING
Five Hour Service

Each of those men had a gun in his hand, and they saw Ed and Chubby at once.

"There's the brat, Mike!" one of them shouted. "I told you the dame sent him for help!"

"Okay!" Mike barked. "Burn them both down!"

The guns of the two men jerked up in unison.

Ed Race was handicapped by Chubby, whom he was holding on his right arm. He swung the lad down to the ground, and gave him a shove which sent him tumbling over toward a set-back in the building. At the same time, Ed dropped to one knee. His left hand flicked in and out from his shoulder holster. His powerful revolver thundered simultaneously with the spiteful bark of the guns in the hands of the two killers.

One of their slugs whined in the air, scarcely an inch from his ear. The other gouged into the cement sidewalk at his side, and ricocheted up into space.

But those two shots were the last the gunmen fired. Ed had scarcely taken the time to aim. Though they were more than seventy feet away, their bulk was certainly vastly larger than that of the glowing end of the cigar he had just hit, on the stage of the Clyde Theatre. He didn't even look to make sure he had struck them. He *knew*. He knew that when those men were examined, a lead bullet would be found in the heart of each of them.

The reverberations of that swift exchange of shots were still echoing down the street when he sprang up and snatched at Chubby's hand.

"Come on, kid!" he shouted, and lifted him to his shoulder, and ran swiftly into the alley between the Clyde Theatre and the office building which adjoined it.

BEHIND THE office building, he made he his way along backyards toward the rear of the building in which Mary Warren's store was located. From what Chubby had told him, he understood that there must be a very good reason why Mary didn't want the police brought into this thing. If he remained to answer questions now, the police would surely take over. There would be plenty of time later, to come back and make explanations. Ed was known to the police, and could afford to take a certain amount of leeway. Inspector MacSpain, the dour head of Homicide, was his friend, whom he had often helped.

For Ed was something more than a star vaudeville performer. That uncanny ability of his with guns, plus a restless nervous energy which craved a constant outlet in excitement, had prompted him to choose an avocation—that of criminology. Ed Race held licenses to operate as a private detective in a dozen states, and his name was as hated in the underworld as the name of the Masked Marksman was admired and applauded in the entertainment world. More than once had he been called upon by his friends of the theatrical fraternity to lend his uncanny ability with guns to the solution of problems of theirs. It was not strange, therefore, that Mary Warren should have thought first of him when danger came.

From the direction of the street, there began to come sounds of police whistles, and of a radio car siren. Ed could imagine the scene out there, with the blue-coats throwing a cordon around the block, hoping to catch the killer of those two hoodlums. It would only be a matter of minutes before MacSpain got there, and that shrewd homicide inspector would not be slow to connect Ed Race with the fact that the killings had taken place outside of the Clyde Theatre. He would learn that Ed had just come out of the Clyde, together with Chubby. MacSpain's next stop would surely be the Warren Photographic Shop. There was no way to avoid that. What Ed hoped to do was to get a few minutes alone with Mary Warren before MacSpain arrived.

In that he was not disappointed, for just as he got abreast of the rear of the store, Chubby pointed upward excitedly toward the apartment window.

"There's Aunt Mary," he said.

She was looking out, and as soon as she saw Ed she waved, and hurried downstairs to open the back door for him.

While they waited, they could hear the sound of her racing footsteps on the wooden stairs, and Chubby nestled close.

"Gee, Uncle Ed," he said with eyes wide and wondering, "you sure can shoot! You—you killed those two bad men, didn't you?"

Ed swallowed hard, and nodded.

"Yes, Chubby, I killed them."

"When I grow up, Uncle Ed, I want to shoot guns like you. Can I? Will you show me how?"

"Yes, Chubby. I'll show you how."

Mary was opening the door for them now, and she stood aside for Ed to enter, then swiftly shut it behind him.

She hadn't turned on any light, and he could hear her gasp in the dark as she took Chubby from him.

"Oh, Ed!" she whispered. "It—it was terrible. I knew you wouldn't fail me. Come upstairs while I put Chubby back to bed. Then—then I must ask a favor of you."

He followed her up, and she said over her shoulder, "I—heard the shooting outside. It was you, wasn't it, Ed? Those two men?"

"Yes," he said. He asked her no questions. And she, on her part, asked him nothing more about the shooting. It took her less than five minutes to get Chubby safely tucked in bed, and Ed Race watched from the hallway. He could see little, because she did not put on a light. But he could just barely make out that the twin bed alongside of Chubby's was empty. The covers were rumpled, mute evidence that Chubby's twin sister, Nora, had lain in it tonight. But Nora was no longer there.

ED SAID nothing. He didn't know whether she knew he had noticed the empty bed. But he did note that Mary Warren refrained from asking him to come in and say goodnight to Chubby. She just asked the little fellow to throw a kiss to Ed, and while the boy did it, she stood in such a way as to screen the empty bed from Ed's view.

Chubby was asleep almost as soon as his curly head hit the

pillow. Ed smiled in the dark. What a happy faculty childhood has, he thought, of shedding all care and worry, and dropping into slumber at a moment's notice. Not even the excitement of running on to the stage of the Clyde Theatre, or of witnessing a gunfight, had been able to keep his weary little eyes open a moment longer. Many a dyspeptic millionaire would have traded all his wealth in exchange for that ability merely to fall asleep!

Mary Warren came out into the hall, and softly closed the door. In the darkness, she took Ed Race's arm, and pressed it.

"Thank you, Ed," she whispered, "for not asking questions!"

Grimly, he went downstairs with her. Down here there was a hall, into which he had come when he entered the building. It ran all the way from the front to the rear, and the front door was open, as those two thugs had left it when they had run out in pursuit of Chubby.

Mary opened a door in the side of the hall, which led directly into the photographic store. There was no light in here, either, and she guided him in the dark by the arm, to the rear, where the darkroom was located.

Out in the street they could see police squad cars, and a milling crowd of people around the bodies of the two gunmen. For an instant, Ed caught sight of the stocky, powerful figure of Detective Inspector MacSpain, issuing crisp orders. Ed nodded in satisfaction. MacSpain hadn't inquired at the Clyde Theatre yet. That would give him a few more minutes of time before the inspector would come here. Time enough to hear Mary Warren's story.

She led him into the darkroom. And not until she had closed

the door tightly, did she turn on a light. And then it was only a small, ten-watt "safelight," used while developing film. In that eerie, uncertain illumination, she turned and faced him.

Mary Warren was a beautiful girl. The top of her auburn hair barely came to his shoulder. And even here it was easy to see that she was holding her slim body under tense control only by a supreme effort of will.

"The police will be here very soon, Ed," she whispered. "They're sure to come when they learn about Chubby going into the Clyde after you." She closed her eyes tightly for a moment. "I—I shouldn't have sent him. But—but I really didn't think clearly. I was too frightened."

"Frightened?" he asked. "Of what?"

She looked up at him only for an instant, and then dropped her gaze.

"Please, Ed—will you do something for me—a great favor—without asking any questions?"

"What is it you want, Mary?"

For answer, she turned to the developing table, which extended along one wall of the darkroom. Set in niches in the table, there were three deep tanks containing developer, chrome alum hardening compound, and acid fixing bath, respectively. Ed knew what was in each of the tanks, and just how they were used, for he had occasionally come here of an evening, before his number went on at the Clyde, and helped Mary Warren develop and print films.

MARY DIPPED her arm deep into the acid fixing tank, and drew out a strip of ordinary 120 roll film. She took it to the sink, and washed it in running cold water, and then hastily rolled it up. She filled a small can with water, put the roll into it and screwed on the cover. She offered it to Ed Race.

"This can won't leak," she said. "I want you to take it to a certain man. That's all. Will you do it?"

Ed raised his eyebrows. "Is that why you routed Chubby out of bed, and sent him down the dumbwaiter? Is that why you told him to get me over here right away?"

"Yes, Ed," she said simply. "It—it's more important than you think. And I can't explain."

He took the can, and held it in his hand. "Who's the man I'm to give this to?"

"His name is Galliani, and he'll be waiting for you in Room six-o-eight of the Mercury Hotel, on Fifty-first Street."

Ed studied her face under the dimly filtered rays of the safe-light.

"Do you realize, Mary, that I just shot and killed two men out in the street almost in front of this store? Do you realize that MacSpain will be looking for me in a short while? Don't you think you should tell me more about this?"

She swallowed hard, and her small fists pressed tightly against her sides.

"I'm sorry, Ed. I—I can't tell you any more. I—I must ask you to do this blindly."

"Suppose the police pick me up while I'm carrying this film?"

She uttered a little cry of consternation. "Oh, God, no! You mustn't let them, Ed. You mustn't. You—you know how to avoid them—"

Ed thrust the can of film into his jacket pocket, and put one big hand on her shoulder. With the other, he lifted her chin up so that he could look down into her eyes.

"Mary," he asked slowly, *"has this anything to do with the fact that Nora's bed is empty?"*

She cringed from him as if he had struck her. "Then you saw—"

"Of course I saw, Mary. And Chubby let something drop, too." His fingers dug hard into her shoulder. "Why can't you trust me, Mary? Don't you owe me that much? Is it because they've taken little Nora away?"

She nodded, biting her lip. "Yes. They've taken—Nora. Galliani made me promise I'd not tell a soul—or I'd never see Nora alive."

"And this film in my pocket is to be the ransom?"

"Yes."

"But why? What's on this film that makes it worth the life of a little girl?"

"I don't know, Ed. I swear, I don't know. Galliani brought it in here tonight, and wanted me to develop it, while he waited. It's panatomic film, and I told him it would take two hours. He wouldn't wait. He seemed terribly nervous, and kept watching the street all the time. He had two other men with him. They all looked—like frightened rats."

"Go on," Ed urged her, tightly.

"They talked among themselves for a few minutes, and then Galliani saw a picture of the twins, and he laughed wickedly. He whispered to his two companions, and they went upstairs and took Nora out of bed, without disturbing Chubby. Galliani said they'd take Nora away with them, and that I was to bring the film over to the Mercury Hotel when it was developed, or send it by messenger. I wasn't to print the pictures, just to develop the film. And that if he didn't get the film by eleven o'clock, I'd never see Nora alive again. They took Nora away with them. And Galliani threatened that they'd kill Nora if I notified the police!"

"I see," Ed said gently. "And what about those two men I just shot?"

"Ten minutes after Galliani and his men left, these other two arrived. They wanted to know what Galliani had been doing here, and if he'd left any film to develop. I lied, and told them he hadn't, thinking they'd go away. But instead, they said they'd stay all night. They got their guns out, and waited for Galliani to come back. I was desperate. If they stayed, I'd not be able to develop the film, and then Galliani would kill Nora. So I went into Chubby's room and woke him up, and sent him down the dumbwaiter to get you—"

SHE BROKE off, gasping as the sound of loud knocking came from the front door of the store. At the same time, they heard heavy footsteps moving down the hall, and then up the stairs to the apartment above.

"The police!" she exclaimed. "If Galliani has someone watching, they'll think I called the police! They'll kill Nora!"

A voice called from upstairs, "There's nobody up here, Inspector, except that little boy, an' he's sound asleep."

"Only one?" they heard MacSpain call. "There should be two—twins."

"No, sir. There's another bed, but it's empty."

"You're sure Miss Warren isn't in any of the other rooms?"

"Nobody else up here, sir."

"All right, Peters, you stay up there. I'll see if I can get into the store."

Inside the darkroom, Mary Warren clutched at Ed Race's sleeve.

"Ed!" she whispered in a panic. "Inspector MacSpain will catch you in here! I left the side door to the hall unlocked. He'll come in and find you. You've got to get away—"

They heard the knob of the side door turning, and then the creak of the hinges, followed by MacSpain's footsteps in the store, just outside the darkroom.

Swiftly, Ed reached over and switched out the safelight. It left him in total darkness. He opened the darkroom door just a crack, and peered out. Inspector MacSpain was barely five feet away. He had a flashlight out, and was throwing its beam around the store, upon the display cases of cameras and photographic materials.

Another detective came in through the hallway, and reported to him.

"We've identified those two muggs, Inspector. They're Ike Sharp, and Patsy Liggio—two of Nick Hawks's trigger men."

"Nick Hawks!" exclaimed Inspector MacSpain. "What were *his* hoods doing here? Anything on them?"

"No, sir. But each had fired one shot. And each of them has a hole in his chest the size of a house. Looks like forty-five slugs."

"I thought so," MacSpain said reflectively, flickering his flashlight around the store. "It's Ed Race's work, all right. No one else could shoot it out so neatly with two hoods like that. The city owes him a vote of thanks. I wonder why he scrammed!"

The detective returned to his duties outside, and Ed remained at the crack of the darkroom door, watching tensely. The mention of the name of Nick Hawks had set his blood racing. Everybody knew that Nick Hawks ran a string of gambling layouts in the city, and that he protected them with a small army of gunmen, like Ike Sharp and Patsy Liggio. But no one had ever been able to prove anything on Hawks. The man lived luxuriously, and ran a chain of cheap picture theatres as a blind for his real operations. He always travelled around with a couple of so-called "assistant managers," who were really bodyguards. But why two of Nick Hawks' gunmen should have come to this little photographic shop to lie in wait for a man named Galliani, Ed couldn't understand.

"What he did know was that Mary Warren was sobbing quietly at his elbow here in the darkroom, knowing that if he was discovered by MacSpain, he would not be able to deliver the film to Galliani, and that little Nora Warren would die as a result.

He saw MacSpain turn slowly, swinging his flash toward the darkroom. Hastily, Ed closed the door. He stood utterly still, feeling the warm, palpitating body of Mary Warren close beside him. Clearly, they could hear MacSpain's steps approaching.

"Ed!" she gasped in a choked whisper. *"What'll we do?"*

Ed pushed her toward the door. "Get out there, Mary," he whispered, "and divert his attention while I sneak out. Act as you never acted before in your life. Do a strip tease if you have to—*but hold his attention!*"

He felt her straighten up beside him. "All right, Ed," she said in a small voice. "Here goes. And—you've *got* to succeed!"

She began to utter a series of queer, choking moans, in a low, strangled voice. At the same time, she shook the doorknob hard.

"Help!" she gagged. "Help!"

Then she turned the knob, and stumbled out of the darkroom, dropping to her knees.

ED NODDED approval as he listened to her act. She was giving it all she had. He heard MacSpain utter an exclamation of surprise, and, peering from behind the door, saw the inspector swing his light down toward Mary.

"Miss Warren!" he exclaimed, stooping to lift her up.

Mary fell into the Inspector's arms. She began to talk hysterically, in a loud voice, to cover any possible noise Ed might make as he stole across the store behind MacSpain's back.

"Robbers! They—they broke in and wanted money. They hit me on the head—" as MacSpain started to turn around, she raised her voice louder, and clung to him so hard that he couldn't move for a moment—"don't leave me! I'm afraid! Help me—water...."

Ed was out in the hall by this time. He heard no more as he stole down toward the rear, and out the back way.

It was only a matter of moments before he was out in the street, and mingling with the crowd which was thronging around the scene of the shooting. The morgue wagon was there, and they were loading the bodies of the two dead gunmen into it.

Police had formed a circle around the spot, and traffic was being pushed through a bottleneck. The congestion was pretty bad.

Ed had left the Clyde without a hat, so he had nothing to shade his face from observation. But he kept to the shadows as much as possible, moving toward Broadway.

He passed two cops who were discussing the shooting, and one of them said, "Sharp and Liggio were plenty tough. But they met someone tougher this time, all right. There's only one guy I know of who could put two slugs in them so neat—and facing their guns, at that!"

"Yeah," said the other cop. "The Masked Marksman. I've seen his act a dozen times. The guy is uncanny. I bet Sharp and Liggio didn't know who they were up against, or they'd have quit before they started. They were just yellow rats."

Ed passed on, and was almost at the corner of Broadway when his eyes suddenly narrowed. Instinctively, his shoulders hunched slightly forward, in the motion which he customarily made when he wanted to bring his holsters into position for a quick draw.

The thing which had made him get set for action was the splendid Rolls Royce limousine which was pulled up in front of the fire plug at the corner. The license number on that limousine was NH—2. Its solid bulk gave the impression of an armored car—which indeed it was. For this was one of Nick Hawks' three cars. Hawks was sitting in the rear, with Gil Smood, his personal bodyguard. In the front seat, beside the chauffeur, sat another bodyguard, whom Ed knew by the name of Jake Longo. He saw that all three of the men were watching him with curious, intent expressions.

There was no question in Ed Race's mind, but that Nick Hawks and his paid killers were in some way connected with that roll of developed but unprinted film in his pocket. The man, Galliani, had brought it to Mary Warren to be developed, and immediately thereafter, two of Hawks' gunmen had come looking for Galliani. They had asked for the film. And here was Nick Hawks himself, in his luxurious limousine, right on the street where two of his thugs had just met death. It must be something vitally important to bring the big boss down here in person. Ordinarily, the loss of two gunmen would not have affected him in the least. As a matter of fact, his usual procedure when his trigger-men got in trouble, was to disavow them entirely—and secretly hire a shyster lawyer to defend them. But when they were killed, he never even admitted that they had been working for him.

Ed came abreast of the limousine, walking with his shoulders slightly hunched forward.

HAWKS, WHO was sitting nearest the curb, opened the window and stuck his head out. His small, basilisk eyes centered upon Ed.

"Hello, Race," he said in a flat, unemotional voice.

"Hello," Ed replied. He kept on walking.

"Wait," said Hawks. "What's your hurry, Race? Let's talk for a minute. You don't want to pass by an old friend without talking—especially when you just knocked off two of his boys!"

Ed stopped, and turned slowly.

"What makes you think I knocked them off?" he asked steadily.

Hawks' grin was like that of a wolf.

"I don't think, Race. *I know!*"

Ed raised his eyebrows. "Getting clairvoyant?"

"Not clairvoyant, Race. Just good eyesight. I saw you shoot them down. My boys, here, saw it, too. We were just turning into the street. Too far away to do anything about it then." He paused, and then added significantly, "But it's not too late to do something about it *now.*"

Gil Smood in the rear, and Jake Longo in front beside the chauffeur, both had their hands stuck in under their coats, touching the butts of their guns, and ready to draw at a word from the boss.

"We'd have every right to shoot you down," Hawks went on. "The cops will find the bullets in Sharp and Liggio came from your revolver. We could say that you attacked us, the same as you attacked them. The cops will believe us—self defense!"

Ed Race's eyes were narrowed slits. His hands hung loosely at his sides. He was watching Smood and Longo, but he spoke to their boss.

"Any time you want to give the word, Hawks, why go ahead. If you think those two rats of yours can get their guns out before I can draw—give them the word. But remember that your face is nearest to me. Have you ever seen me do my act? Have you ever seen how fast I draw? *For instance—*"

His hands moved in a sudden blurred flurry of motion which was impossible to follow. And, magically, he was holding the two

.45 caliber, hair-trigger revolvers—one pointing past Hawks' face at Smood, the other pointing obliquely at Longo, in the front.

The two gunmen were caught absolutely flat-footed. Their own guns had barely had a chance to start coming out of the holsters. Their faces went a sickly green, and they sat frozen, incapable of moving. Hawks, too, remained transfixed, his face framed by the window of the Rolls Royce.

Ed smiled thinly. Almost as swiftly as he had produced the twin revolvers, he returned them. In the short space of four seconds, he had drawn his guns, kept those men covered for enough time so that they could feel the fear of death, and then had returned the weapons to their holsters. His hands hung loosely at his sides once more. The whole thing had been so swift, that no one in the street even noticed what had happened.

"And now, Mr. Hawks," Ed said softly, "do you want to let your boys try again? Maybe they'll be a little faster next time."

Smood and Longo hastily took their hands out from under their coats—empty—and put them in their laps. They wanted no part of the Masked Marksman—face to face.

Nick Hawks swallowed hard, and wiped sweat from his forehead. "God!" he said. "You're a damned wizard!"

"Thank you," Ed said. "And now—do you mind if I leave? I wouldn't advise you boys to shoot me in the back when I walk away. You couldn't very well call *that* self-defense!"

"Wait a minute!" Hawks said urgently. "Hold on, Race. I'd like to talk business with you."

"Well?"

HAWKS STUDIED him for an instant. "A rat named Galliani used to work for me. He was a croupier at one of my dice games. He brought some film to the Warren dame tonight, to develop. I want that film. I'll give you twenty-five grand for it!"

Ed smiled, shook his head. Even if he had needed the money, he wouldn't have considered trading—with little Nora Warren's life in the balance. But he had made plenty of money in his vaudeville career, so that he was well-fixed for life. And Hawks knew that. It indicated the desperation to which the gambling king was being driven, that he made this offer, which he knew would not be accepted.

"Sorry, Hawks," Ed said.

The other's eyes became cagey. "Then you have the film?"

"None of your damned business. And now, good-by!"

Ed Race turned on his heel, and continued on toward the corner. He had learned something, but still not enough. One thing he had learned for certain—that the film in his pocket was of supreme importance to Nick Hawks—of so much importance that the gambling king might even now be desperate enough to give his gunmen the order to shoot Ed in the back, in an effort to recover it.

He did not turn around, however, but kept on, at an even pace, toward the corner. In his mind, he tried to picture himself in Hawks' position. If the man was desperate enough to order Smood and Longo to shoot, it would take him a moment or more to arrive at the decision. Hawks would probably try to figure his chances of beating the rap for such a shooting, would probably decide that since the police were now looking for Ed, there might be some legal justification for shooting him—even in the back. So about now, he might be giving the okay. Smood and Longo would be getting out of the car, pulling their guns....

He was at the corner. He turned left on Broadway, and involuntarily looked backward, tensing for a quick draw if it should prove necessary.

He was almost disappointed that he hadn't figured it right.

Hawks must have evolved a different plan. For the limousine was no longer at the curb. It was moving out into traffic, in the opposite direction. Ed couldn't see inside the car, so he didn't know whether Hawks and Smood and Longo were still in it, or whether they had gotten out in order to follow him on foot. But he was sure that Hawks hadn't given up. That roll of film was too important.

Ed walked swiftly up Broadway now, toward Fifty-first. It would be necessary for him to double on his trail and make sure he wasn't followed, before going to see Galliani at the Mercury Hotel. Nothing must be permitted to endanger the safety of little Nora. He thought of Mary Warren, back at the photographic shop, bravely answering the hammering questions of Inspector MacSpain, probably enduring a grilling.

This thing had happened so suddenly tonight, that he had not had much opportunity to consider his own position. He had definitely compromised himself with the police, by disappearing after the shooting. True, MacSpain had said that the town owed him a vote of thanks for killing Sharp and Liggio. But the District Attorney, who was not a friend of his, might not take such a broad view of it. Ed's duty as a citizen was to have remained right there and explained that he had fired in self-defense, and to have offered little Chubby Warren's testimony in evidence of that statement. But he hadn't done it that way. And he was sure, in addition, that the film in his pocket would be of definite value to the police. Otherwise, Hawks would not have been so interested in getting his hands on it.

AT FORTY-SEVENTH STREET, Ed turned and looked behind him, but could not spot anyone following him. That did not mean that he was not being tailed. Hawks, or Longo, or Smood—or all three of them—could be on the opposite side of the street, or they might be tailing him in a taxicab. He decided to take a cab himself, and ride around the town a little—and then he looked at a clock in a jeweler's window, and changed his mind.

It was five minutes of eleven!

Time had passed much faster than he had thought. And Mary had told him that if the film was not delivered to Galliani at the Mercury Hotel by eleven o'clock, Nora Warren would die! There was no time to shake any possible followers. He must go straight ahead, regardless of consequences. He hastened his steps up Broadway, and turned swiftly into Fifty-first.

The Mercury was a second-grade hotel, with not much of a lobby. Hangers-on of the underworld patronized this place. Touts, tipsters, drug peddlers, made it their headquarters. Murder had taken place in this hotel on several occasions in the past, and each time it had changed names. But it remained the same sort of hotel, nevertheless.

Ed made straight for the elevator, and pressed a five-dollar bill into the hand of the operator. "Go straight up," he said. "Don't wait for any more customers!"

The operator glanced at the denomination of the bill, and said, "You bet!" Just as the door closed, Ed saw Smood and Longo come into the narrow lobby, half running. Behind them, he glimpsed Nick Hawks.

Smood and Longo waved for the cage to wait for them, but the boy pretended not to see their signal, and closed the door all the way. The cage shot upward.

"What floor, mister?"

"Twelve," Ed said.

The operator glanced at him over his shoulder, and grinned. "There ain't but eight floors in this here hotel, mister."

Ed looked sheepish. "All right. Make it eight."

At the eighth, Ed got out. He took out a twenty dollar bill, and tore it in half. He gave one half to the boy, and put the other back in his pocket.

"Take your time going down," he said. "If you can make the down trip last about five minutes, so those bozos can't ride up, I'll give you the rest of that bill when I come out."

"*If* you come out!" the operator said gloomily.

"I generally do!" Ed told him.

The boy grinned, and nodded. "Okay, mister. It's a sale."

He closed the door, and Ed saw the cage move down very leisurely, past the glazed door. As soon as he was alone, Ed streaked for the stairs, and hurried down to the sixth floor. He found 608 without trouble, and rapped hard.

He must have been expected, for a voice close to the other side of the door called hoarsely, "Yes? Who?"

"It's about—the film," Ed said.

"You got it with you?"

"Yes."

Immediately, the lock was turned, and the door came open.

A SHORT, wizened man with a pinched face, and the eyes of a cornered rat, was standing just inside. He had a big automatic in his hand, and pointed it straight at Ed's stomach.

"Come in," he said. His eyes watched Ed unblinkingly, and he wet his lips nervously with his tongue.

Ed walked into the room.

There was no one else in the room. The little, wizened man closed the door and locked it, keeping Ed covered.

"All right," he said. "Hand over the film."

Ed shook his head. "Not yet, Galliani."

"What do you mean?" snarled the other.

"Where's the little girl—Nora Warren?"

"She's okay. You gimme the film. If it's right, the kid will be returned."

"No," said Ed.

Galliani grinned wickedly. "Mister, you ain't smart. Nobody in this here hotel will pay any attention to a shot. You hand over that film, or I give it to you in the guts and take it!"

He thrust the gun forward, and raised it a little, so that the muzzle was centered on Ed's breastbone. "And no more talk. It's the film—or curtains!"

"You're wrong," Ed said mildly, "about nobody paying attention to a shot. There are three men in this hotel right now, who will be very much interested. Would you like to know who they are?"

"Nuts to you!" snarled Galliani. "I told you I don't want no talk—"

"The names of these three men," Ed went on imperturbably, "are Hawks and Smood and Longo. Interested?"

Galliani's eyes widened. His mouth went open for a second, and then he shut it, his lips twisting into a sneer. "To hell wit' that. *You* didn't bring them. They'd of taken the film off you—"

"Not from *me,*" Ed told him. "Here's the film. I'll show it to you, just to prove I've got it. But I don't hand it over till I get little Nora Warren—alive and safe!"

As he spoke, he put his hand in his pocket. His coat tightened across his chest and Galliani said, "I see the bulge of your guns, pal. If your hand touches one o' them under the coat, I'm pulling the trigger!"

Ed smiled, and brought the can out. He opened it, and extracted the roll of film, under the other's eagle eye.

"Now to prove it's the right film..." with one hand he held up the film and let it unroll, while with the other he closed the can and put it in his breast pocket.

Galliani's eyes were no longer on that hand. They were fixed with deadly earnestness upon that film. He kept his automatic trained on Ed's chest, and reached with his free hand for the roll.

Ed's eyes flickered. His hand, under the coat, was no longer holding the can. It was gripping the butt of a .45 caliber revolver. And while Galliani reached for the film, Ed's hand came out.

That lightning motion was so swift that as far as Galliani

was concerned, it might never have happened. All he knew was that something seemed to flicker past his face, and then there was a stunning crack against his gun wrist. The automatic fell out of his hand. Every nerve of his arm was paralyzed, as far up as the elbow.

HE STOOD there stupidly, looking at the roll of film still suspended in Ed's hand.

Ed kicked the automatic over into a corner, and then shoved Galliani into the single chair in the room.

"If you move," he said to the stunned rat, "I'll crack you over the skull!"

Galliani was too dazed even to be frightened. He just sat where Ed had thrust him, still not fully comprehending that he had lost the upper hand.

Ed holstered his revolver, and took this opportunity to examine the roll of film. It was the first chance he had gotten since coming into possession of it.

There were six exposures, and they all had all been taken in broad daylight, somewhere on a roof top. Whoever had taken the pictures had stood on one roof, and had focused on a scene taking place on an adjoining roof. He must have snapped them in quick succession, for they represented a single continuity of action.

And it was the character of that action which caused Ed Race to utter an ejaculation of complete understanding. The first exposure showed the figure of a man coming up through the skylight of the building, carrying an inert body on his shoulder. The second, third and fourth showed him carrying that body across the roof to the parapet. The fifth was a distinct picture clicked just as the man was in the act of hurling the inert body over the parapet. His back was to the camera here, but in the sixth exposure his full face showed as he walked back from the parapet toward the skylight.

And even in the negative it was easy to identify that man—Nick Hawks!

Ed looked up from the film, to see Galliani eyeing him covertly.

"Who's the victim?" he asked, tapping the roll of celluloid.

"None of your damn business," Galliani snapped, nursing his broken wrist.

Ed watched him shrewdly. "I could guess. Three or four months ago, there was an item in the papers about a wealthy young man named Blaisdell, who committed suicide by jumping from the roof of Nick Hawks' Casino Club. At a guess, I'd say that Blaisdell must have got in an argument with Hawks, and that Hawks hit him too hard, and killed him. So he took him up to the roof and dumped him, making it look like suicide!"

He saw Galliani sort of shrink into himself as he listened, and Ed knew he had guessed right. Galliani must have taken these pictures, and had probably tried to blackmail Hawks. But in order to make sure, it had been necessary to develop them. Galliani and his gang of rats, knowing too little about developing to do it themselves, had brought the pictures to Mary Warren. And they had taken little Nora as hostage, to make sure they'd get their film back.

No wonder Nick Hawks wanted that roll so badly!

Grimly, Ed thrust the roll back into his pocket, and went over and seized Galliani by the collar.

"All right," he said. "Talk fast. Where's the little girl—Nora Warren?"

"You go to hell!" said the rat-faced man.

"No," Ed said. "J won't go to hell yet. *You* will!"

He lifted Galliani off the chair by his coat collar, and fairly dragged him over to the window. He hoisted him up, one hand on his collar, the other on the seat of his pants, and forced him out over the sill.

"Here you go," he said. "*This* will look like suicide, too. But there's nobody to take pictures of it!"

"Wait!" shrieked Galliani. "I'll talk!"

Ed held him over the sill. "Talk, then!"

"You—you won't throw me out if I talk?"

"Not if the girl is safe!"

"She's safe, all right. Sam and Pete—my two pals—got her down in room three-o-one. It's the truth, so help me!"

"All right," Ed said grimly. "We'll see." He dragged Galliani inside, held him up with his left hand, and hit him hard on the jaw with his right. The rat-faced man crumpled like a spineless puppet. Ed let him down to the floor, not bothering to tie him. It would be a long time before he came to. He stepped over the inert man, yanked open the door, and stopped short.

Gil Smood and Jake Longo were standing in the hallway just outside the door, with guns in their hands, and grins on their murderous faces. Behind them, Nick Hawks was standing with a long-barreled Luger.

LONGO AND Smood pulled the triggers on their guns almost at the instant when Ed opened the door. But Ed's powerfully muscled body, trained to instantaneous response to reflex action, went into a bewildering back flip, away from the door, and over toward the left.

If Smood and Longo had kept their guns in line when they fired, they couldn't have helped hitting Ed Race, no matter how fast he moved, for the speed of a bullet from a modern automatic cannot be beaten by anything known to man. But that perplexing back somersault had tricked more than one expert killer in the past, as it did them. They swerved their guns in an effort to follow him, and in so doing they lost their target. Their slugs smashed into the plaster.

They never got a chance to fire a second shot, because Ed Race was back on his feet at the far side of the room, with his two hair-trigger .45's belching flame and thunder in streams of deadly fire.

Smood and Longo went down, backward, their bodies smashing into Nick Hawks, who was directly behind them. But Ed didn't stop shooting. Grimly, he triggered those two revolvers, sending slug after slug into the falling bodies. Those bullets smashed through the bodies of Smood and Longo, and hit Hawks. One of them took him square in the heart, and he was dead when he landed on the floor.

Ed Race's guns were empty when he stopped shooting.

Grimly, slowly, he crossed the room and stepped over the three dead men, out into the hall.

He was just in time to meet Inspector MacSpain and two detectives, who came barging out of the elevator.

"By God!" exclaimed MacSpain. "I knew if we followed Hawks, he'd lead us to you! Eddie, I've got to arrest you—"

"Wait a minute, Mac!" Ed interrupted. "Take a look at these!"

He thrust the films into the Inspector's hand, and MacSpain whistled when he saw them. Ed let him look.

"Get down to three-o-one," he told the two detectives. "There are two rats down there, holding little Nora Warren. You better get more men, and try to take them from the window!"

Less than ten minutes later, little Nora Warren was safe in Ed's arms, in the lobby of the Mercury, and Galliani and his two accomplices were being led into a Black Maria.

"I guess," Inspector MacSpain said with a twinkle in his eye, "that I can pass up arresting you for the shooting of those two lugs on Forty-Sixth Street. I don't think the D.A. will want to prosecute, when he hears the story."

"Thanks for nothing!" Ed grumbled. "What a pal!"

MacSpain sputtered with mock indignation. "Here I am, giving you every consideration, and you keep on grumbling! What more do you want?"

"A police car with a loud siren," Ed told him, "to help me get Nora back to her Aunt Mary and her twin brother—and I mean *right now!*"

MacSpain's eyes twinkled. "I'll take you myself, Eddie. I want a chance to find out more about this photography business. There seems to be something to it!"

MURDER'S ONE-MAN SHOW

CHAPTER 1
GIRL IN THE GALLERY

THE GIRL was wearing a neat, tailored blue suit and a high-necked blouse of white silk. She was dark-haired, her legs were shapely, and she was slim and attractive.

Ed Race noticed all these things about her as she came running down the steps of the Lawrence Art Gallery on Fifty-seventh Street. He stopped short on the sidewalk, because he saw that if she continued down at the speed with which she was coming, she would bump into him. She couldn't see Ed, because she was looking behind her as she ran.

Ed wondered what there could be inside of the Lawrence Galleries which could have frightened her so. And then she tripped on the next to the last step, and fell right into his arms.

Her body was soft and fragrant, but she suddenly squirmed and fought like a little wildcat. Ed could see that she was both startled and terrified, and that her violent effort to get free was a reaction from the suddenness of her fall into his arms. He grinned, and set her down on her feet. She was breathing hard, and throwing apprehensive glances back toward the entrance of the Lawrence Galleries.

She straightened her coat, and smoothed down the disarranged blouse over her heaving bosom, and then smiled up uncertainly at Ed.

"Oh—I—I'm so sorry. I was startled—"

San Toro said, "You weel not shoot, Señor Race. Observe where I hold thees gun!"

"That's all right," said Ed.

Impulsively, she put a hand on his arm. "Would—would you help me?"

"If I can."

Once more she threw a hasty glance toward the doorway out of which she had come running. "A—a nasty man was annoying me—in there. He's following me out. Would—would you—stop him?"

"Of course," Ed told her. "Here he comes now. You run along, and I'll just give him a little lecture—"

He stopped, and began to grin once more. The man who had been pursuing the young lady appeared in the doorway and came down the stairs on the run. And Ed knew him by sight. He was Second Grade Detective Joe Griscomb, attached to the Forty-seventh Street Police Station. The Clyde Theatre, where Ed staged his Masked Marksman show twice a day, was in this precinct, and he knew every one of the plainclothesmen in the

district. Twice a day he startled the packed audiences of the Clyde with the wizardry of his gun-juggling and marksmanship act. But outside the theatre, he had another avocation which had often brought him in close touch with the police.

That avocation was criminology. He held licenses to operate as a private detective in a dozen states, and his friend, Inspector MacSpain, had often said that Ed attracted trouble the way jam attracts flies. Truly, he had often found worthy use for the two heavy forty-five calibre hair-trigger revolvers which he always carried in his shoulder holsters.

But tonight, he wasn't sure whether this was going to be comedy or tragedy. He was quite sure that Detective Joe

Griscomb hadn't tried to force his attentions on this girl—pretty though she was. For Griscomb was a young detective who was head-over-heels in love with his new bride.

Ed looked down at the girl, studying her quizzically.

"So!" he said. "This is the man who was annoying you, eh?"

"Yes!" she gasped. "Please keep him here till I get away—"

She started to run, and Detective Griscomb shouted, "Hey, Mr. Race! Hold her!"

HE TOOK the rest of the steps down to the street in a flying leap, and Ed grasped the girl's arm. She tried to twist out of his hold, but Griscomb reached her and put a hand on her shoulder.

"All right, young lady," he growled. "You're under arrest!"

He turned to Ed. "She just stole a picture out of the gallery. Cut it out of the frame with a razor blade. There was a painting stolen last week, too, and I was watching for the thief to come back and try again!"

The girl stamped her foot angrily. "That's ridiculous! I'll sue you! How dare you accuse me of stealing a picture? You can see I haven't anything—"

She turned appealingly to Ed. "Don't believe a word he says. He was trying to date me up, in there, and now he's trying to make a lame excuse. Think of it—accusing *me* of being a thief!"

Her face was flushed, and her eyes flashed angrily—so angrily that Ed was tempted to believe her innocent.

But Joe Griscomb laughed harshly. "That painting was only ten inches square. It's a nude by that new artist, Pasquale Manuel. It's worth fifty thousand dollars. You tucked it somewhere in your clothes. Lady, you're going to be searched by a matron!"

He reached for her handbag, which was tucked under her arm.

"Here. Let's see what's in here—"

Griscomb's hand was still on her shoulder, and as he took the bag out from under her arm she suddenly bent her head and sank her teeth in the fleshy part of his hand. The detective gasped with the sudden pain, and yanked his hand away.

The minute she was free, the girl turned and ran.

Griscomb cursed under his breath, dropped the purse, and started after her.

The purse fell to the ground at Ed Race's feet. Ed didn't join in the pursuit. He felt that Joe Griscomb should be amply able to handle that girl, and the purse presented a subject of greater interest at the moment. For two cars had just come cruising down the street. They were both gray, two-door coaches, and alike as two peas, including license plates muddied over so to be indistinguishable. One of these cars pulled in at the curb, while the other kept going in the direction of the fleeing girl and Joe Griscomb.

Out of the car which had stopped, there stepped a tall, distinguished looking gentleman in a Prince Albert, with striped pants and a cane. He wore a moustache and a goatee, and had the appearance of a Spanish grandee, or of a foreign ambassador. This gentleman hurriedly stooped to pick up the purse which the girl had dropped.

The purse was half a dozen feet from Ed, quite close to the

curb. Ed's eyes narrowed. He stepped forward quickly, and put his foot on the purse, just as the foreign looking gentleman was about to grasp it.

"Better leave it alone, mister," Ed said mildly.

The gentleman straightened up, frowning, without lifting the purse. "Excuse, please," he murmured. "You weel kindly to take thee foot from thee purse. Eet ees thee purse of my wife, which she 'ave drop."

Ed raised his eyebrows. "You mean to say that little girl who's running away is your wife?"

"But yes, señor. An' now—"

He stooped once more to pick it up.

Ed kept his foot on it. "You know," he said, "I think you're a liar!"

THE FOREIGN looking gentleman muttered an oath. He turned to the car from which he had descended. A swarthy fellow, also in a Prince Albert, was sitting at the wheel.

"Juan," the bearded gentleman said to this swarthy one, "thees man 'ere—'e make trouble!"

Juan's lips parted in a grin. "Oho! We shall see!" His hand rose from the cushioned seat, gripping a huge, wide-mouthed revolver. He swung it toward Ed.

Now, for the first time, Ed Race began to take more than an impersonal interest in the proceedings. His reaction—at first—had been the same as that of a bored man-about-town at a summer resort, who suddenly spots a pretty girl in the hotel. Only with Ed, it was the scent of danger which provided the stimulus. Ed could appreciate a pretty girl as well as the next man. But give him the choice between the charming company of the most beautiful woman in the world, and a night spent matching wits and guns with the underworld of crime—and Ed would always choose the latter.

It was one of the reasons why he had never married. For he knew in his heart that if a call came from a friend at crime's mercy on his wedding night, he'd forsake the honeymoon.

So now, when he saw the big gun in Juan's hand, it was almost with a feeling of pleasure that he went into action.

The chances were that neither Juan nor the bearded gentleman were able to tell just what happened. On the stage of the Clyde Theatre, the Masked Marksman gave a nightly demonstration of the same swift draw which he now executed. He did it while going into a back somersault, with his hands empty. The audience usually let out a long gasp of surprise when they saw him coming back on his feet—with a gun in each hand. Then they gasped again as the two guns blasted out thunderously, snapping out the flames of a row of candles, thirty feet across the stage.

So perhaps Juan uttered a gasp when he saw the flicker of motion made by Ed's hand, and then felt the searing thud of a bullet into the fleshy part of his shoulder. Certain it is that he never saw the heavy forty-five come out of the holster.

Ed fired only once, to disable the man. At the same instant, be thrust out with his left hand against the chest of the bearded gentleman, sending him sprawling into the side of the car. Then he stooped and snatched the purse from the ground. He had no fear that Juan would pick up the revolver and shoot with his left hand, for he knew just how much shock can be conveyed to a man's body by the impact of a forty-five calibre slug.

He stuffed the purse in his pocket, and at the same time he heard the staccato *rat-tat-tat* of a machine gun around the corner. The girl had disappeared around that corner, with Joe Griscomb chasing her—and so had the second of the two identical cars.

Ed cursed under his breath, and set off at a run toward the corner.

The rattle of the machine gun ceased suddenly and was replaced by a woman's scream. Ed couldn't be sure, but he thought he recognized the voice of that girl. He sprinted forward, and a bullet fanned his cheek from behind. Ed didn't even turn to look. He wanted to get around the corner and see what had happened to Joe Griscomb.

The girl's scream was repeated once more, while he was still twenty feet from the end of the block. And at the same time, a second bullet whined through the air, almost biting his shoulder. Indeed, it came so close that he thought the cloth of his coat must be scorched.

Still, he did not take the time to turn and shoot back. Either Juan, or the bearded gentleman with the Spanish accent, was trying to get him in the back, and the next try might be a good one.

His legs were ramming up and down like pistons when he rounded that corner—just in time to see the gray coach roaring away down at the far end of the block, with the door swinging open, and two figures struggling, half inside and half out on the running board. One of them was a thick-set man, and the other was the girl who had stolen the painting. The thickset man was trying to drag her inside, and the girl was trying to break his grip and jump from the racing car.

CHAPTER 2
ED RACE—KILLER!

THE GIRL was mad, for if she did break the stocky man's hold, she would go catapulting from that speeding auto with an impetus that would surely smash her body to pulp.

Ed could have hit that man easily with a snap shot, even in the moving car. His narrowed eyes were centered on the fellow's mop of black hair which hung down over his forehead as he struggled with the girl, and Ed could have put a bullet right square in the center of his forehead. But to do so would have meant certain death for the girl, as well. So he held his fire, and the next instant the car had swung around the corner and was gone.

Ed turned swiftly to the body of Detective Joe Griscomb, lying in a pool of blood on the sidewalk.

The single burst of machine gun slugs had filled the young detective's chest full of lead. He would never again come home to his bride.

A gust of fury swept through Ed Race. Whoever these picture crooks were, they had not hesitated to kill in order to recover their loot. For the sake of a piece of canvas ten inches square, young Joe Griscomb was lying dead now, and his new bride was a widow.

Ed whirled to retrace his steps around the corner. There might be a chance yet to catch Juan and the bearded man. But he had hardly taken two steps before a siren screamed almost in his ear, and a police car raced up alongside him with squealing brakes and scorched tires. A police sergeant leaped out of the car with service revolver in hand, and leveled it at Ed.

"Drop that gun, you!" he barked. "Drop it or I'll drill you!"

Ed froze where he was. He could understand the sergeant's mistake. There was the dead body of Joe Griscomb on the ground, and here was he, with a revolver in his hand.

Ed knew this fellow. He was Luke Morrison, who had recently been transferred to the precinct from the headquarters squad, and who was so officious and blustering that he had made himself obnoxious to everybody in the district.

"I can't drop this gun, Morrison," Ed said. "You know damned well it's a hair-trigger. If I drop it, it'll go off."

Morrison came forward, peering at Ed's face.

"Oh," he grunted. "So it's you, is it? Who'd you kill this time?"

He bent for a moment over the body of Griscomb, and then straightened, his beefy face growing purple. His eyes became specks of rage.

"So you're a cop-killer now, huh!" he came over and extended his hand, palm up, at the same time pointing his service revolver at Ed's stomach.

"Let's have that gun of yours!"

Ed did not surrender his forty-five. Instead, he deliberately returned it to its holster.

"Don't be a fool, Morrison," he said in a low voice. "You can see that poor Griscomb was killed by a machine gun—"

"Yeah," said Morrison. "I see. I also see that you were scramming away from here when we pulled up. Daly saw you scramming, too!" He jerked his head in the direction of Patrolman Daly, the driver of the police car, who had scrambled out by this time.

Sergeant Morrison kept his eyes on Ed, but spoke over his shoulder to the patrolman. "You're a witness, Daly. You saw him running away."

"That's right, Sergeant," Daly said reluctantly. "But Mr. Race is no murderer. He's a friend of Inspector MacSpain—"

"Never mind that!" Morrison exploded savagely. "MacSpain is on vacation, and can't do him any good. The fact is, we caught him in the act of running away from the scene of a murder. That's enough to hold anybody on—"

"Damn it, Morrison," Ed protested, "I was trying to catch the killer's accomplices. There were two cars—"

"Sez you!" Morrison sneered. "Suppose it was the other way around? Suppose you were in cahoots with the killer—"

"You're crazy!" Ed exclaimed. "I can prove what I say. There was a girl whom Joe Griscomb was after. She stole a painting out of the Lawrence Galleries around the corner, and Joe chased her—"

He stopped, his eyes widening in amazement. Coming from around the corner, there appeared the gentleman in the Prince

Albert, with the moustache and the goatee. He was carrying a gold-knobbed cane now, and he was hurrying. At sight of the group around Griscomb's body, he waved his cane and shouted, "Ah! I see zat you 'ave catch thee criminal! *Bueno!*"

MORRISON MOVED around a little, so he could see the new arrival, and still keep Ed covered.

"Who're you?" he demanded.

The bearded gentleman bowed from the hips. "Permit me! I am thee Señor Felipe de San Toro. My apartment—eet ees opposite to thee Lawrence Galleries. From my window I 'ave see 'ow thees man—" indicating Ed—" 'ave snatch thee purse of a woman, an' thee detective 'ave chase 'im. Then 'ave come thee car weeth thee machine gun, an' thees man 'ave call to those in the car to shoot thee detective. Thee detective 'ave start to run around thees corner, but those een thee car 'ave keel 'im. I 'ave become dress very queek, an' 'ave come down to tell all thees!"

"Ah!" Morrison said triumphantly. "Thanks very much, Mr. Sam Toro. You don't know how much I appreciate this!" He smirked at Ed. "Well, Mr. Masked Marksman, what have you got to say now? Here's a man who testifies he saw you give the word to gun Griscomb!"

"He's a damned liar!" Ed exclaimed. "He's one of the crooks. The girl stole a painting from the Lawrence Galleries, and then San Toro's accomplices killed Joe and kidnaped the girl—"

"But no!" interrupted San Toro. "I am insult'! 'E 'ave taken thee purse of the woman!"

Morrison eyed Ed narrowly. "What about that, Race? Have

you got the purse? If you have it, you might as well admit it, because you'll be searched."

"Good Lord!" Ed protested. "You can't believe a cock-and-bull story like that—"

"*Your* story sounds more like cock-and-bull," Morrison broke in. "Now answer yes or no—*have you got that purse?*"

Ed sighed. "Yes—"

"Aha! So you admit everything! You're under arrest—"

"Wait, Morrison! I tell you, that girl stole a painting, and Griscomb was chasing her. This San Toro was in a car with another man, whom I shot—"

"Well, well!" Morrison sneered. "So now you admit you shot some one!"

"Certainly. You didn't give me a chance to explain—"

"You'll have all the chance you want—before a jury! Come on, now. We'll check on this fairy tale of yours about a girl stealing a painting from the Lawrence Galleries!" He took Ed's arm in a steely grip, and motioned to San Toro to come along. "Stay here," he ordered Daly, "and keep the crowd from touching the body."

A small crowd had gathered, and they watched in silence as Morrison led Ed Race around the corner, with the Señor Felipe de San Toro talking volubly, explaining how shocked and horrified he had been at witnessing the brutal attack in the street.

Ed Race refrained from talking. He saw that it was useless to attempt to make any explanations to Sergeant Morrison. Whatever he could say would be a waste of time. The only thing that would tend to support his story would be the missing picture in the gallery.

The Lawrence Galleries seemed to be entirely quiet and undisturbed by the events which had taken place. It was a private salon for the exhibition of paintings, and there were never many people there at any one time. Their sales ran into large sums of money, so that they did not need to do a volume of business.

There was a short hall, which opened directly into the exhibition gallery, and at the doorway to the room there was a small gilt sign which read, PLEASE RING FOR ATTENDANT.

Morrison grunted, and stuck a thumb on the bell. They heard it ringing somewhere in an inner office. The exhibition room contained perhaps thirty oil paintings, and fifteen or twenty etchings, displayed artistically along the walls. Ed glanced around swiftly, trying to spot the empty frame from which the girl had cut the small canvas. But he was interrupted by the appearance of Westley Lawrence, the proprietor, from the rear office.

CHAPTER 3
JOE GRISCOMB'S WIDOW

LAWRENCE WAS a small, bird-like man with large blue eyes, and a weak chin. He smiled ingratiatingly when he saw Señor Felipe de San Toro, but frowned in the direction of Ed and Morrison, as if wondering what these interlopers were doing in the sacred precincts of his premises. "Ah, Señor de San Toro," he exclaimed. "It is indeed a pleasure to see you tonight. I hope you have decided to purchase the Manuel. At fifty thousand dollars, I assure you it is an unqualified bargain—"

Señor de San Toro waved his hand deprecatingly.

"Later, Señor Lawrence. We 'ave another matter now."

He turned to Morrison. "You see, eet ees that I am a good customer of Señor Lawrence. In Spain, I 'ave a great art collection. I buy many paintings een thees countree—"

"Never mind that now," Ed broke in. He addressed the gallery proprietor. "Look here, Mr. Lawrence. Did you have a detective guarding these premises."

Lawrence frowned, and nodded. "Indeed, yes. There was a Detective Griscomb here, but I do not see him. A painting was stolen last week, and I asked for a police guard—"

"How about the painting that was just stolen?" Race demanded. "A small one, ten inches square, and worth fifty thousand dollars!"

Lawrence jerked to attention. "Stolen? My God! That would be the Manuel—the one I'm trying to sell to Señor San Toro. Stolen, you say? Impossible. Let me see—"

He hurried across the room, with the others trailing him. On the far wall, with a small electric light bulb directed upon it, hung the smallest oil painting Ed had ever seen. It was enclosed in a simple black frame, and depicted a nude dancer about to do a pirouette, with her arms high in the air. Every line of the dancer's slim and supple body expressed grace and beauty, and movement. There was something almost ethereal about her body, which was creamy white and pink against a background of rich purple draperies.

"You see!" exclaimed Westley Lawrence. "It is not stolen." He wagged a finger in Ed's face. "What sort of nightmares do you dream? Who told you it was stolen?" He turned around to San Toro. "Here it is, Señor de San Toro, in all its beauty. The smallest canvas in the world, by the newest genius among painters, Pasquale Manuel. See the perfection of detail, the magnificence of the color—" Ed wasn't listening. He was staring, almost incredulously, at the painting. This was it, without a doubt, for Griscomb had said that it was ten inches square, and this one exactly fitted the size. Had Griscomb lied then? Or were there two such paintings in the Lawrence Galleries?

But far overshadowing even that conjecture in Ed's mind, was another fact—*the nude dancer in that painting was the girl who had fallen into his arms a few minutes before!*

The face which peered out at him from that rich miniature canvas was the face of that girl. And if he was any judge of feminine form, the body was hers, in size and contour. She had posed for this picture!

Ed ran a hand over his forehead. The girl had certainly been running away when she fell into his arms, off the gallery steps. Joe Griscomb had accused her of stealing this portrait, and to avoid being searched she had bitten the detective's hand and run away. And yet—here was the picture, intact! Was it possible that the girl had been telling the truth, and that Griscomb had really been trying to annoy her?

He snapped to attention as Sergeant Morrison produced a set of handcuffs.

"Well, Mr. Masked Marksman, it looks like you're in this thing, right up to your neck! Your story has been proved a lie, all the way down the line! First you claim that Mr. San Toro, here, was in with the killers, and it turns out he's a wealthy man and a customer of the Lawrence Galleries. Then you claim a girl stole a picture, and it turns out that the picture is right here!" He thrust out the handcuffs. "Let's have your mitts, Mr. Masked Marksman! You're going in the can—on a charge of complicity in murder!"

ED RACE had never been one to kid himself. He saw the seriousness of his situation now. Morrison would, of course, have to establish a motive on Ed Race's part, if he wanted to convict him of being involved in the killing of Joe Griscomb. But Ed knew just how they would handle a man in headquarters, who was accused of killing a cop. Also, he was beginning to feel that this case would take a little high-powered investigating on his part. He realized that he was up against a pretty clever man in the person of the Señor Felipe de San Toro. In jail, Ed wouldn't have the ghost of a chance to get to the bottom of the queer business. And in the meantime, who could tell what would happen to that girl? He was sure that she had been kidnaped by San Toro's accomplices. Whether she had stolen a picture or not, he didn't know right now. But he meant to find out.

So the first thing that happened while Morrison was extending the handcuffs, was that Ed's hand seemed to make a *whirring* motion in the air, and suddenly, the barrel of one of his heavy forty-fives was descending upon Morrison's wrist.

He didn't hit any too hard, because he was reluctant to do permanent damage to a cop—even to one like Morrison. But the blow was sufficient to smack the revolver out of the detective sergeant's hand. Then, almost in the same motion, Ed brought the forty-five up, and the barrel clicked lightly against the point of Morrison's chin. The sergeant's head jerked back, and his eyes glazed. His jaw went slack, and he toppled slowly forward.

Ed caught him, and eased him down to the ground, then sprang up. His idea was to get Señor de San Toro off by himself somewhere, and give the Spanish gentleman a thorough grilling.

But Señor de San Toro was apparently no slouch as far as quick thinking went. He had no desire, it seemed, to be present in the same room with Ed Race—without the protection of the police. While Ed was lowering the unconscious form of Morrison to the floor, San Toro turned and ran headlong out of the exhibition room, shouting with all the power of his lungs.

"'Elp! Police! Thee murderer 'ave escape'!"

Westley Lawrence stood ringing his hands in panic, and staring wide-eyed at the big gun in Ed's hand. San Toro's voice came rumbling back to them from the street, shouting ever higher and higher.

Ed cursed under his breath. There would be other policemen out there now, and they'd be swarming in here in a moment. He swung the gun on Westley Lawrence, making his face as ferocious as possible.

"I'm a desperate man, Lawrence," he growled. "Do you want me to put a slug right in your guts?"

"N-no! P-please—"

"All right then. Show me the back way out of here—quick!"

Shaking all over, Lawrence led him through the rear, and out to the back entrance. Already, there were the sounds of running footsteps at the front of the building, and Ed could hear San Toro's voice.

" 'E mus' be escape by thee back way—"

Ed gripped Lawrence's arm tightly. "Look here," he demanded. "Are you sure nothing was stolen from the gallery tonight?"

"Y-yes!" the little man quaked. "N-nothing was t-taken—"

"Are you sure that Manuel painting is the original? Sure it wasn't switched?"

"I—I didn't look c-carefully. B-but it seems to be the same—"

"All right. I want you to go and examine it with a microscope. I'll call you on the telephone, in a half hour. Let me know what you find out. And remember—if you tell the police I'm going to 'phone you, I'll come back and blast your front teeth into the back of your head!"

Making his face look as murderous as he could, he shoved Lawrence backward into the hall, and sprang out of the back door into the rear alley, just as San Toro's voice came more clearly than ever from the exhibition room.

ED SPED along the alley, and as he got out into the next street, he caught the high-pitched voice of Westley Lawrence yelling that the murderer had threatened to fill his guts with lead.

Ed grinned thinly in the darkness. He crossed the street, cut through another alley, worked over toward the avenue, and hailed a cab. He gave an address on Ninety-fourth Street, which was where Joe Griscomb lived.

As the cab sped uptown, Ed took the purse from his pocket

and examined it. He whistled when he saw the contents. He had thought that possibly he might find the folded canvas in here, but there was no stolen painting in the purse. It contained a driver's license and a passport, both in the name of Georgette Vaughn. The picture on the passport was that of the girl who had posed for the Manuel painting—and who had been accused by Joe Griscomb of stealing it.

In addition to the usual feminine accessories, there was a roll of bills containing almost nine hundred dollars, and a checkbook on the National City Bank. The address of Georgette Vaughn was given in the driver's license as the Greymont Towers, on Fifty-seventh Street, which was one of the swankiest residence buildings in town. There was also a small, engraved calling card, with a beautiful crest in one corner, and the name: *"Señor Felipe Miguel de San Toro y Moroja."*

On the back of the calling card there was scribbled: *"Lawrence Galleries, 10 P.M.—we shall await you outside, dear lady, and protect you!"*

There was no signature to this gallant note but Ed's eyes flickered. He was willing to bet that the handwriting would turn out to be that of Señor de San Toro.

Ed put all the things back in the purse, with a perplexed frown creasing his forehead. The name of Georgette Vaughn was familiar to him. He recalled that she had been in the newspapers on numerous occasions. Her maiden name had been Georgette Ross, and she had been a sort of madcap debutante a couple of years ago. The papers usually had a good time recording her pranks. Then she had married the millionaire, Roger

Vaughn, and had gone on leading a careless and expensive life. Ed remembered hearing one of the gossip columnists on the radio report that Georgette was now separated from her husband. It was quite believable that she would pose in the nude for a Spanish painter. She was bound by no conventions. But he couldn't imagine her trying to steal the picture later.

He remembered vividly now, the moment when he had rounded the corner and seen her struggling in the car with the stocky man whose black hair came down over his forehead. There was no doubt that she had been kidnaped—either for ransom, or for the purpose of getting that portrait, which they must also have believed she had stolen. San Toro must have tried to get the purse, just to make sure she hadn't hidden it in there. Or, perhaps, he had merely wanted to get his card back. That card might be valuable later.

The cab stopped in front of the apartment house where Joe Griscomb lived, and just then the radio switched from music to a news announcer: "... *Ed Race, a vaudeville actor, wanted jor complicity in the murder* of *Detective Griscomb... police are working on the case....*"

ED LET the radio go on. He told the driver to wait, and took the self-service elevator up to the fourth floor. The door of 4-C was unlocked. Under the bell there was a neatly typed card bearing the name, "Griscomb." Ed could hear Mary Griscomb in the foyer, talking on the telephone. Her voice was choked with emotion.

"Is—is he—dead? Please tell me... I can't believe it... Ed

Race? God, no. Ed was Joe's friend… you're sure, Sergeant Morrison? All right—I—I'll come right downtown…."

Ed heard her hang up and utter a choked sob. He pushed the door open and stepped into the foyer.

Mary Griscomb was standing, white-faced and taut, at the telephone table. She had been married only three weeks—and now she was getting the news which policemen's wives live constantly in dread of hearing. Her eyes widened at sight of Ed Race, and her hands clenched. "You!" she said. Ed came in slowly.

"Yes, Mary. It's I. They—told you about Joe?"

"They—told me."

"They said I killed him?"

"They said you—are responsible. Morrison has a witness—who heard you order the machine gunner to shoot Joe down!"

Ed came a little closer to her. "Mary, do you believe that? Do you believe I had anything to do with killing Joe?"

Her breast was heaving, and her fingernails were biting into the palms of her clenched hands. She was making a terrible effort to control herself.

For a long tense, minute, she looked straight into Ed's eyes, looked deep and searchingly, with all the poignant discernment of a bereaved woman. At last she took a deep breath.

"No, Ed," she whispered. "I—don't—believe it!"

Ed breathed a deep sigh. Gently he took her arm, and led her to a seat in the living room. Then he told her the whole story of how Joe Griscomb had died—omitting nothing. She listened, dry-eyed, tense, every fibre of her trembling. When he was done, she closed her eyes, sat that way for a long minute. Then she opened them, and looked straight at him.

"What are you going to do, Ed?"

"I'm going to find that black-haired man. I'm going to find where they've taken Georgette Vaughn. I'm going to get the goods on San Toro, and prove he's the brains behind the conspiracy—whatever its purpose!"

"But—but how can you do all that—with the police on your trail?"

"I'll do it, all right! It'll be hard. With MacSpain away on his vacation, there's no one I can go to, in the department. I can't ask anyone else to take a chance on being involved with me. Mac would do it, without my asking twice. But now—I'll have to work alone."

"Not alone, Ed," Mary Griscomb whisperer. "I'm going with you. I'm going to help you find Joe's murderer!" She stood up, and there was fire in her eyes. "I'm sure Joe would want me to do it—rather than go down to the morgue and look helplessly at his body. I'm sure that's the way a policeman's wife should act!"

Ed pressed her hand. "Good girl!"

Together they went downstairs.

CHAPTER 4
PENTHOUSE TRAP

THERE WAS no longer a crowd in front of the Lawrence Galleries. The body of Joe Griscomb had been removed from around the corner, and only one uniformed policeman stood on guard in front of the Gallery entrance.

Ed told the cab driver to stop a little further up the block, and pointed out to Mary Griscomb the apartment house across the street, where Señor de San Toro had said he resided.

They got out, telling the cab driver to wait again, and walked swiftly toward the building. It was a small, remodeled house, with two flats on a floor. The names in the bells indicated that San Toro lived in an apartment on the first floor.

Mary followed Ed upstairs, and he carefully tried the door. It was locked. He whispered instructions to Mary, and she nodded understanding. He backed against the wall, out of sight of anyone opening from within, and Mary knocked diffidently on the door.

There was no answer, and she knocked again.

This time there was the sound of movement from within, and a muffled voice demanded, "Well? Who?"

"It—it's about the picture," Mary said, through the door. "I must see you at once, Señor San Toro."

There was a grumbled response, and the door came open a crack.

Mary bent and peered through the crack; and whispered, "There's no chain. Ed."

"Good!" Ed said. He came out from alongside the wall, and hurled his weight at the door.

Surprisingly, it gave easily before his onslaught, as if the party on the other side had taken the precaution to step out of the way.

Too late, Ed knew he had thrust himself into a trap. He went hurtling into the hallway, and someone clicked a switch, and the light went on.

Detective Sergeant Morrison's gleeful voice said, "All right, Race, I knew you'd show up here sooner or later. Get your mitts up!"

A bitter feeling of failure throbbed through Ed Race's pulse, even as he went stumbling forward down the length of the hall. He should have known better than to come here. Morrison had outguessed him. He had expected to find only San Toro, and perhaps some of his murderous friends here. Instead, he found that Morrison had been lying in wait for him. And where he would have been eager to shoot it out with San Toro and his friends, he could not shoot at Morrison. If he allowed himself to be captured now, San Toro would have the field all to himself. With Georgette Vaughn in his hands, the wily Spaniard could proceed to frame a perfect case against Ed, and at the same time accomplish his own ends without hindrance.

Ed had trained himself to think clearly and accurately while in violent motion. It had been necessary to acquire this facility, because both accuracy of judgment and of marksmanship were demanded in the act which he performed daily in the theatre. When he went into a back or forward somersault on the stage, he had to keep his mind clear in order to enable him to judge distances to a hair's breadth—so that when he came out of the somersault, he could place his shots exactly where he wanted them.

Now, as he stumbled ahead, he sent his powerfully muscled body into a forward somersault. Morrison's shout was still ringing in his ears, and he knew that Morrison's service revolver was trained on him, and would probably begin to blast within another second. But he also knew that he must take this chance in order to escape—that if he did not make a break for freedom now, he'd never have another opportunity. So he kept going forward, into the somersault.

MORRISON YELLED, *"Hey!"* and pulled the trigger of his revolver. The first shot went high, as it usually did when anyone fired at the Masked Marksman in motion. That trick somersault always fooled them. But Morrison was a crack shot, and he couldn't fail to miss on the second or third try. Ed hoped only that he would not be hit in a fatal spot. The hall was a long one, and there was ample time for Morrison to fire twice or three times more before Ed could reach the doorway at the far end. Of course, he could have drawn his own gun and killed the detective sergeant with a single shot. But that was a thing he would not allow himself to do.

He executed three forward somersaults which brought him up to the door, expecting each moment to hear the explosion of the detective's gun, and to feel the hot slug bury itself in his body. But no more shots came. He heard the sounds of a scuffle, and as he came to his feet he saw that Mary Griscomb had leaped upon Morrison, and had wrapped both arms around the detective's body, pinning his hands to his sides.

Morrison was struggling viciously, but Mary Griscomb held on with the grip of desperation, and she managed to gasp, "Keep going, Ed! I'll—hold—him!"

Ed's eyes were shining with admiration. "Nice going, Mary!"

he called back, and leaped into the next room. He heard the two of them struggling in the hall as he raised one of the windows, and scrambled down the fire escape. In a moment he was out in the street, and was climbing into his taxicab.

"Uptown," he ordered. "Greymont Towers, on Fifty-seventh Street!"

Just as the cab completed its U turn and started north, Ed looked back out of the rear window, and saw Morrison come barging into the street, waving his gun. He shouted after the cab, but Ed's driver didn't see him, and turned the next corner, unconcernedly.

"Make it snappy," Ed told him. "I'm in a hurry. It's worth five dollars extra for me to get there in ten minutes.

"Right!" the driver said enthusiastically, and stepped on the gas.

The cabby thought he was just earning an easy five, but in reality he was pulling away from the squad car in which Morrison had started to give chase. Without knowing it, the driver was doing an excellent job of showing his heels to the law.

When they reached the Greymont Towers, Ed saw that the clock showed seven-sixty. With the extra five he had promised the driver, it made a total of twelve-sixty. He gave the man fifteen dollars, and told him to wait, with the flag up.

"Mister," said the cabby, "at this rate I'll wait for you till Hitler gets to America!"

Ed nodded, and hurried away from the cab, to the entrance of the Greymont Towers. It was impossible for him to put into so many words the reasons for coming here. Partly, it was cold logic, but to a greater extent it was a combination of hunch and character analysis. From what he had seen of Señor Felipe de San Toro, he judged that old Spanish rogue to be a man of great cleverness and of cool daring. He had seen how de San Toro had invented a story on the spur of the moment, in order to put Ed at a disadvantage. And he now had a glimmering of the depths of the conspiracy which he was sure de San Toro had fathered. Therefore, he was morally certain that the Spaniard would continue to act in a daring and original manner. If he was wrong, he would have to give up and take his medicine—primarily consisting of one whale of a beating at the hands of Morrison, down in the third-degree room.

Ed stepped into the beautiful stone entrance of the Greymont Towers, and almost bumped into a uniformed doorman.

"What floor for Georgette Vaughn?" Ed demanded.

He had expected that the doorman would be frigid, and refuse him admittance. Instead, the fellow nodded respectfully, and said, "Mrs, Vaughn occupies the penthouse, sir. Follow me to the penthouse elevator."

CHAPTER 5
ED'S MASTERPIECE

ED BEGAN to feel a little trickle of premonition as he followed the doorman across the lobby. The fellow was certainly acting out of character. He had never seen a flunky in so swanky an establishment who had not acted superciliously, and who offered to usher a visitor up without announcing him from the foyer.

"It's a self-service elevator, sir," the man told him, holding open the door of the cage. "Just go in, and press the penthouse button."

"Yeah?" said Ed. "Don't you have to announce me?"

"Oh, no, sir," the man smiled eagerly—almost too eagerly. "Mrs. Vaughn is expecting you."

"Expecting *me?* Do you know my name?"

"Why certainly, sir. You are Mr. Edward Race. I was told to send you right up if you arrived."

"You don't say!" Ed murmured.

The doorman seized the door, ready to swing it shut as soon as Ed entered the cage.

Ed ducked low, grasped the man's arm, and then pivoted on his heel. He got the fellow's arm over his shoulder, and heaved. The doorman went flying over Ed's head, and landed square in the cage, on his hands and knees. He uttered a shrill curse, and scrambled to his feet, with blood pouring from his nose. But Ed slammed the door shut, and nodded in satisfaction.

Upon stepping toward the cage, the door itself had been open, so that he had not been able to observe it. But he had seen a stout staple in the jamb—a staple which should never have been present in the door of an elevator. Now he saw that there was a stout padlock hanging by a hook on the door. He slipped the padlock over the staple on the doorjamb, and clamped it shut, just as the doorman inside hurled himself against the door.

"Lemme out!" the fellow yelled.

Ed grinned. "Just press the penthouse button," he called.

He waited, watching the indicator. Nothing happened. He nodded to himself. That elevator cage had been fixed so that it wouldn't work. The power must have been disconnected, so that it could neither rise nor drop. Once inside that cage, with the padlock securely fastened on the outside, Ed would have been a helpless prisoner until it suited his captors' fancy to release him—or turn him over to the custody of the police.

The doorman inside kept banging against the metal door, and Ed let him. He walked across the lobby to the main elevator. There was a little service closet alongside the elevator shaft, also with a padlock on it. Ed tried the lock, but it would not open. He took out one of his revolvers and fired a single shot into the staple. The explosion reverberated throughout the lobby, and must have sounded to the tenants in the building like the back-fire of a huge truck. But the staple flew off, and the door of the closet swung open. Ed looked in, and grinned.

The real doorman of the Greymont Towers, and the elevator boy, were lying in there, trussed up, with gags stuffed into their mouths. They stared up at him in fright.

Ed smiled at them. "I'll just leave the door open, so you can get some air, boys," he said. "I haven't the time to untie you now. Wait'll I get down again."

He left them there, and stepped into the main elevator shaft. He slid the door shut, and pulled over the lever. This elevator worked all right, and the cage shot straight up to the penthouse.

Ed hunched his shoulders forward, so that the twin forty-fives in his holsters leaned out, ready to be grasped and drawn instantly. He opened the door and stepped out on to the roof.

The Vaughn penthouse was ablaze with light.

Ed hurried up the paved walk, between two small plots of smooth lawn, and stopped at the front door. The Venetian blinds were drawn all the way down, so he couldn't see inside the two windows facing on the lawn, but he could hear the sound of voices within, particularly the accented voice of Señor Felipe de San Toro. He couldn't distinguish what was being said, however.

Suddenly, above the sound of those voices, he heard a woman's scream. It wasn't a scream of pain or agony—but one of protest, perhaps of terror.

ED WAITED no longer. He put his hand on the knob, tried the door and found it locked. He turned his gun down on the lock, stepped back, and fired four times into it. The powerful sledgehammer blows of those forty-fives literally thrust the whole door backward tearing the tongue of the lock from the slot. Ed kicked the door wide, and sprang inside. He crossed the foyer in a single bound, and burst into the living room.

His hunch had been right! With the clever daring of the super crook, Señor Felipe de San Toro y Moroja had chosen the home of Georgette Vaughn in which to hold her prisoner. Technically, no one could call it kidnaping to bring a captive to her own home!

Georgette Vaughn was in a straight-backed chair in the center of the room. The black-haired man who had dragged her into the fleeing car had hold of one of her arms, and Juan had hold of the other. Juan had his coat off, and a bandage around his shoulder, where Ed had shot him. Behind the chair stood Señor San Toro, with a gun in his hand. They had taken off Georgette's jacket and skirt and blouse, and she was clad only in a pink slip. San Toro had her jacket in his hand, and had been slitting it open with a kitchen knife, which he dropped at Ed's precipitate entrance, in favor of a gun.

The black-haired man, who was holding on to Georgette's left arm, reached into a shoulder holster for a gun, but San Toro's cold, calm voice interposed.

"It weel not be necessary, Manuel. Have no fear. Señor Race weel not shoot us!"

Ed had both revolvers in his hands, one trained on Manuel, the other on Juan. By a quick, sure movement, he could have shot San Toro, too. But he saw what the wily Spaniard meant when he said there was nothing to fear. San Toro had placed the muzzle of his own gun at the back of Georgette Vaughn's neck, and was holding it with his finger curled around the trigger.

"Observe," he said dispassionately, "where I hold this gun, Señor Race. Eet ees true that you are what-you-call, *wiz-ard* weeth those rai-volv-air. But observe too, that I can pull thees trigger weethout effort. Should you begin to shoot, the so-beautiful Madam Vaughn mus' die!"

"I see," Ed said slowly. Georgette Vaughn had ceased struggling with the two men who held her. She was staring with wide eyes at Ed Race.

"Please—shoot!" she begged. "I—don't want to live any more!"

Ed studied the four of them with narrowed eyes. "These men have been blackmailing you?" he asked her.

"Yes. Manuel here, is a painter. He painted a portrait of me—just a head. I—never posed for the nude. But he painted another nude, and then put my face on it, and they put it up for sale at Lawrence's. They—they wanted me to pay fifty thousand dollars for it, because if Roger, my husband, had ever seen it, he'd surely have divorced me."

"I see," said Ed. "And then, when you refused to pay, along came the Señor San Toro, and told you he'd help you, eh? Told you he'd arrange it so you could go in there and steal the picture?"

"Yes, yes. That's right."

"But San Toro and these mugs just wanted you to get yourself in deeper. They had a detective stationed there, figuring he'd catch you, and then Lawrence could refuse to prosecute—provided you bought the picture you'd tried to steal!"

SAN TORO smiled thinly. "You 'ave thee vairy sharp mind, Señor Race. You 'ave guess' the plan. But now—you can guess that which weel 'appen to Madam Vaughn—onless we can find thee picture w'ich she 'ave taken. We search 'er clothes. Eet mus' be 'ere. Eef not—then eet mus' be in 'er purse—which you 'ave."

"But the picture is right there in the Lawrence Galleries," Ed said, keeping his guns high and level, waiting for the main chance. If ever San Toro should withdraw that muzzle from Georgette's neck for only a fraction of a second....

San Toro laughed. "That picture which is now there, eet ees a duplicate, which my Manuel 'ave made. I replaced eet, while you argue weeth those dumb detective Morrison. Thus, you 'ave been made to seem a liar!"

"Not bad," Ed said. "Now suppose you give Mrs. Vaughn her

clothes again. We're all through playing games. I'm starting to shoot in exactly thirty seconds!"

San Toro shook his head. "Spanish gentlemen and American gentlemen do not endanger a ladee's life. You weel not shoot. On the contraree—you weel 'elp us to find thee painting!"

"Oh, what's the use!" Georgette Vaughn exclaimed. "I give up. It's in the lining of my skirt. I had a false pocket made, and slipped it in there. Now—you can have the portrait, and show it to my husband. I—I'm too tired to fight—"

Juan let go of her arm, and pounced on the skirt. He ripped the lining away, and drew out the small canvas.

"Oho! Now you shall pay—"

"Here goes!" Ed exclaimed, and fired.

San Toro had been so overcome by excitement that he had leaned forward past Georgette's chair, and his gun hand had pushed out forward just an inch or two. It was enough for Ed, and San Toro's wrist crumpled under the blast. Manuel and Juan stood frozen, not daring to move.

Suddenly, Georgette Vaughn uttered a cry. "Behind you—"

Ed heard a foot scrape at his back, and went into a split-second somersault just as a shot crashed from a doorway to the rear. He came to his feet, glimpsing the thin and emaciated face of Westley Lawrence in the doorway. Ed fired while he was himself still a blur of motion, and he didn't bother to look in Lawrence's direction any more, because he knew that he had aimed for the man's forehead, and he always hit exactly where he aimed.

He swung on one knee, his gun thundering in the room as Juan and Manuel began pumping shots at him.

There was a cool, hard smile on Ed's face as he triggered those two guns of his, shooting carefully, accurately, with no more emotion in his eyes than if he had been shooting at a row of candles on the stage of the Clyde Theatre. These men were not only thieves, they were murderers. They had cold-bloodedly machine-gunned a young cop. Ed felt like an executioner as he pumped lead into the hearts of those two men.

He straightened to his feet, with the walls still sending back the echoing reverberations of his thunderous gunfire.

Georgette Vaughn sprang to her feet, then reeled and would have fallen, if Ed hadn't caught her.

"Get your clothes on," he growled. "This is no time to faint or to have the heebie-jeebies. There'll be cops here in a minute."

HIS PROPHECY was pretty accurate as to time. It was only about ninety seconds before the front door banged open, and Detective Sergeant Morrison barged in, with Mary Griscomb at his side, and a couple of plainclothesmen at his back.

Ed tautened, but he relaxed when he saw that Morrison was putting his gun away instead of turning it on him.

Mary Griscomb smiled. She had hold of Morrison's elbow.

"I made him promise not to blow up till he could hear your story, Ed," she said. "I'm just holding on to his arm for insurance. He had to promise, or I wouldn't have told him your plan."

"Swell kid!" Ed praised.

He saw that Georgette Vaughn had got her clothes on, after a fashion, and let her tell her story to Morrison. The wounded San Toro stared impassively, while she talked, then he shrugged his shoulders.

"I 'ave lose!" he said. "Eet seem that I am too smart for mysel'!"

Detective Sergeant Morrison scratched his head, and looked shamefaced.

"Well, I'll be damned! You were telling the truth all the time, Race!" He stuck his hand out. "I apologize."

Ed nodded somberly, and took his hand. Then he turned to where Mary Griscomb had gone into a corner by herself. Now that the tension was over, she was sobbing quietly, with her head on the shoulder of Georgette Vaughn.

Morrison sighed. "Damned lousy—the life of a cop's wife!"

"I'm thinking the same!" Ed Race said.

POPULAR HERO PULPS  AVAILABLE NOW:

THE SPIDER

- ❑ #1: The Spider Strikes $13.95
- ❑ #2: The Wheel of Death $13.95
- ❑ #3: Wings of the Black Death $13.95
- ❑ #4: City of Flaming Shadows $13.95
- ❑ #5: Empire of Doom! $13.95
- ❑ #6: Citadel of Hell $13.95
- ❑ #7: The Serpent of Destruction $13.95
- ❑ #8: The Mad Horde $13.95
- ❑ #9: Satan's Death Blast $13.95
- ❑ #10: The Corpse Cargo $13.95
- ❑ #11: Prince of the Red Looters $13.95
- ❑ #12: Reign of the Silver Terror $13.95
- ❑ #13: Builders of the Dark Empire $13.95
- ❑ #14: Death's Crimson Juggernaut $13.95
- ❑ #15: The Red Death Rain $13.95
- ❑ #16: The City Destroyer $13.95
- ❑ #17: The Pain Emperor $13.95
- ❑ #18: The Flame Master $13.95
- ❑ #19: Slaves of the Crime Master $13.95
- ❑ #20: Reign of the Death Fiddler $13.95
- ❑ #21: Hordes of the Red Butcher $13.95
- ❑ #22: Dragon Lord of the Underworld $13.95
- ❑ #23: Master of the Death-Madness $13.95
- ❑ #24: King of the Red Killers $13.95
- ❑ #25: Overlord of the Damned $13.95
- ❑ #26: Death Reign of the Vampire King $13.95
- ❑ #27: Emperor of the Yellow Death $13.95
- ❑ #28: The Mayor of Hell $13.95
- ❑ #29: Slaves of the Murder Syndicate $13.95
- ❑ #30: Green Globes of Death $13.95
- ❑ #31: The Cholera King $13.95
- ❑ #32: Slaves of the Dragon $13.95
- ❑ #33: Legions of Madness $12.95
- ❑ #34: Laboratory of the Damned $12.95
- ❑ #35: Satan's Sightless Legion $12.95
- ❑ #36: The Coming of the Terror $12.95
- ❑ #37: The Devil's Death-Dwarfs $12.95
- ❑ #38: City of Dreadful Night $12.95
- ❑ #39: Reign of the Snake Men $12.95
- ❑ #40: Dictator of the Damned $12.95
- ❑ #41: The Mill-Town Massacres $12.95
- ❑ #42: Satan's Workshop $12.95
- ❑ #43: Scourge of the Yellow Fangs $12.95
- ❑ #44: The Devil's Pawnbroker $12.95
- ❑ #45: Voyage of the Coffin Ship $12.95
- ❑ #46: The Man Who Ruled in Hell $13.95
- ❑ #47: Slaves of the Black Monarch $13.95
- ❑ #48: Machineguns Over the White House $13.95
- ❑ #49: The City That Dared Not Eat $13.95
- ❑ #50: Master of the Flaming Horde $13.95
- ❑ #51: Satan's Switchboard $13.95
- ❑ #52: Legions of the Accursed Light $13.95
- ❑ #53: The City of Lost Men $13.95
- ❑ #54: The Grey Horde Creeps $13.95
- ❑ #55: City of Whispering Death $13.95
- ❑ #56: When Thousands Slept in Hell $13.95
- ❑ #57: Satan's Shakles $14.95
- ❑ #58: The Emperor From Hell $14.95
- ❑ #59: The Devil's Candlesticks $14.95
- ❑ #60: The City That Paid to Die $14.95
- ❑ #61: The Spider at Bay $14.95
- ❑ #62: Scourge of the Black Legions $14.95
- ❑ #63: The Withering Death $14.95
- ❑ #64: Claws of the Golden Dragon $14.95
- ❑ #65: The Song of Death $14.95
- ❑ #66: The Silver Death Reign $14.95
- ❑ #67: Blight of the Blazing Eye $14.95
- ❑ #68: King of the Fleshless Legion $14.95
- ❑ #69: Rule of the Monster Men $16.95
- ❑ #70: The Spider and the Slaves of Hell $16.95
- ❑ #71: The Spider and the Fire God $16.95
- ❑ #72: The Corpse Broker $16.95
- ❑ #73: The Spider and the Eyeless Legion $16.95
- ❑ #74: The Spider and the Faceless One $16.95
- ❑ #75: Satan's Murder Machines $16.95
- ❑ #76: The Spider and the Pain Master $16.95
- ❑ #77: Hell's Sales Manager $16.95
- ❑ #78: Slaves of the Laughing Death $16.95
- ❑ #79: The Man From Hell $16.95
- ❑ #80: The Spider and the War Emperor $16.95
- ❑ #81: Judgement of the Damned $17.95
- ❑ ***NEW:*** #82: Dictator's Death-Merchants $17.95

THE WESTERN RAIDER

- ❑ #1: Guns of the Damned $13.95
- ❑ #2: The Hawk Rides Back from Death $13.95
- ❑ #3: Gun-Call for the Lost Legion $13.95
- ❑ #4: The Law of Silver Trent $13.95
- ❑ #5: The Gun-Prayer of Silver Trent $13.95
- ❑ #6: Silver Trent Rides Alone $13.95

CAPTAIN SATAN

- ❑ #1: The Mask of the Damned $13.95
- ❑ #2: Parole for the Dead $13.95
- ❑ #3: The Dead Man Express $13.95
- ❑ #4: A Ghost Rides the Dawn $13.95
- ❑ #5: The Ambassador From Hell $13.95

DR. YEN SIN

- ❑ #1: Mystery of the Dragon's Shadow $12.95
- ❑ #2: Mystery of the Golden Skull $12.95
- ❑ #3: Mystery of the Singing Mummies $12.95

THE MASKED MARKSMAN

- ❑ #1: Death Takes an Encore $16.95
- ❑ #2: Death's Understudy $16.95
- ❑ #3: Death Steals the Act $16.95
- ❑ #4: Top Billing for Murder $16.95
- ❑ ***NEW:*** #5: Curtain Call for the Corpse $17.95

POPULAR HERO PULPS  AVAILABLE NOW:

OPERATOR 5

- ❑ #1: The Masked Invasion $13.95
- ❑ #2: The Invisible Empire $13.95
- ❑ #3: The Yellow Scourge $13.95
- ❑ #4: The Melting Death $13.95
- ❑ #5: Cavern of the Damned $13.95
- ❑ #6: Master of Broken Men $13.95
- ❑ #7: Invasion of the Dark Legions $13.95
- ❑ #8: The Green Death Mists $13.95
- ❑ #9: Legions of Starvation $13.95
- ❑ #10: The Red Invader $13.95
- ❑ #11: The League of War-Monsters $13.95
- ❑ #12: The Army of the Dead $13.95
- ❑ #13: March of the Flame Marauders $13.95
- ❑ #14: Blood Reign of the Dictator $13.95
- ❑ #15: Invasion of the Yellow Warlords $13.95
- ❑ #16: Legions of the Death Master $13.95
- ❑ #17: Hosts of the Flaming Death $13.95
- ❑ #18: Invasion of the Crimson Death Cult $13.95
- ❑ #19: Attack of the Blizzard Men $13.95
- ❑ #20: Scourge of the Invisible Death $13.95
- ❑ #21: Raiders of the Red Death $13.95
- ❑ #22: War-Dogs of the Green Destroyer $13.95
- ❑ #23: Rockets From Hell $13.95
- ❑ #24: War-Masters from the Orient $13.95
- ❑ #25: Crime's Reign of Terror $13.95
- ❑ #26: Death's Ragged Army $13.95
- ❑ #27: Patriots' Death Battalion $13.95
- ❑ #28: The Bloody Forty-five Days $13.95
- ❑ #29: America's Plague Battalions $13.95
- ❑ #30: Liberty's Suicide Legions $13.95
- ❑ #31: Siege of the Thousand Patriots $13.95
- ❑ #32: Patriots' Death March $14.95
- ❑ #33: Revolt of the Lost Legions $14.95
- ❑ #34: Drums of Destruction $14.95
- ❑ #35: The Army Without a Country $14.95
- ❑ #36: The Bloody Frontiers $14.95
- ❑ #37: The Coming of the Mongol Hordes $14.95
- ❑ #38: The Siege That Brought Black Death $16.95
- ❑ #39: Revolt of the Devil Men $16.95
- ❑ #40: The Suicide Battalion $16.95
- ❑ #41: The Day of the Damned $16.95
- ❑ #42: The Dawn That Shook the World $16.95
- ❑ #43: When Hell Came to America $16.95
- ❑ #44: Invasion From the Sky $16.95
- ❑ #45: The Winged Horror of the Yellow Vulture $17.95

G-8 AND HIS BATTLE ACES

- ❑ #1: The Bat Staffel $13.95

CAPTAIN COMBAT

- ❑ #1: The Sky Beast of Berlin $13.95
- ❑ #2: Red Wings For the Blood Battalion $13.95
- ❑ #3: Low Ceiling For Nazi Hell Hawks $13.95

ACE G-MAN

- ❑ #1: The Suicide Squad Reports for Death $14.95
- ❑ #2: Coffins for the Suicide Squad $14.95
- ❑ #3: Shells for the Suicide Squad $14.95
- ❑ #4: The Suicide Squad in Corpse-Town $14.95
- ❑ #5: Wanted–In Three Pine Coffins $14.95
- ❑ #6: The Suicide Squad's Dawn Patrol $14.95
- ❑ #7: Targets for the Flaming Arrow $16.95

DUSTY AYRES AND HIS BATTLE BIRDS

- ❑ #1: Black Lightning! $13.95
- ❑ #2: Crimson Doom $13.95
- ❑ #3: The Purple Tornado $13.95
- ❑ #4: The Screaming Eye $13.95
- ❑ #5: The Green Thunderbolt $13.95
- ❑ #6: The Red Destroyer $13.95
- ❑ #7: The White Death $13.95
- ❑ #8: The Black Avenger $13.95
- ❑ #9: The Silver Typhoon $13.95
- ❑ #10: The Troposphere F-S $13.95
- ❑ #11: The Blue Cyclone $13.95
- ❑ #12: The Tesla Raiders $13.95

MAVERICKS

- ❑ #1: Five Against the Law $12.95
- ❑ #2: Mesquite Manhunters $12.95
- ❑ #3: Bait for the Lobo Pack $12.95
- ❑ #4: Doc Grimson's Outlaw Posse $12.95
- ❑ #5: Charlie Parr's Gunsmoke Cure $12.95

THE MYSTERIOUS WU FANG

- ❑ #1: The Case of the Six Coffins $12.95
- ❑ #2: The Case of the Scarlet Feather $12.95
- ❑ #3: The Case of the Yellow Mask $12.95
- ❑ #4: The Case of the Suicide Tomb $12.95
- ❑ #5: The Case of the Green Death $12.95
- ❑ #6: The Case of the Black Lotus $12.95
- ❑ #7: The Case of the Hidden Scourge $12.95

THE SECRET 6

- ❑ #1: The Red Shadow $13.95
- ❑ #2: House of Walking Corpses $13.95
- ❑ #3: The Monster Murders $13.95
- ❑ #4: The Golden Alligator $13.95

CAPTAIN ZERO

- ❑ #1: City of Deadly Sleep $13.95
- ❑ #2: The Mark of Zero! $13.95
- ❑ #3: The Golden Murder Syndicate $13.95

RED FINGER

- ❑ #1: Second-Hand Death $24.95

www.ingramcontent.com/pod-product-compliance
Lightning Source LLC
LaVergne TN
LVHW050645100826
845148LV00011B/1988

* 9 7 8 1 6 1 8 2 7 8 9 8 2 *